IT WAS NEVER US

DROP OF BLOOD

FATEMA M SAIFY

Contents

CHAPTER ONE

THE CRIMSON DAWN

A deep rumble shook the air as red lightning crackle across the sky. In the pitch-black alley, blood poured from the white house above, like a crimson waterfall. Flames danced around the building, forming a fiery barrier above it. In the centre, a woman in red stood, her body pulsating with energy that seemed to radiate outward, illuminating the alley. A chilling wind howled around her, carrying the faint scent of smoke and sulphur.

"Edward, wake up. Something's wrong," Dr. Will said, his voice filled with concern.

Edward gasped, his heart pounding in his chest. It was the same dream he'd had ten years ago, when he was sixteen. The memory was so vivid, it felt like he was reliving it.

They began preparing for research on antidote H, a substance never created before. The stakes were high, and the world was counting on them.

In a dark, deserted alley, Ada stood with her mother, a wise and ancient woman with eyes that held the secrets of the universe. Her mother handed her a glowing red stone, a symbol of her power and heritage.

"Never let go of this," she said, her voice filled with urgency. "Your life depends on it."

With a heavy heart, Ada's mother closed the portal to the upper world, a realm of magic and wonder. Ada then transformed herself into a human named Claire Harper, a young woman with piercing blue eyes and flowing brown hair.

It was the first day of the biology class, and Claire, a fourth-year student, entered the room. The students were immediately drawn to her, their eyes wide with curiosity and a hint of awe. As the class began, Claire sat alone, feeling isolated and out of place. But then, Casper, a kind and gentle boy, approached her and asked ," can I sit beside you".

Before she could answer, the teacher started the class, her voice cutting through the silence. Claire felt a surge of anxiety, but she tried to focus on the lesson.

After class, Claire went to see Uncle Louis. He reassured her, telling her not to worry and to focus on her mission, for what she came here for.

Long ago, people who failed to please or work for the Supreme Spirit were banished to Earth for 200 years. This was a cruel and unjust punishment, and the people suffered greatly. In desperation, the merchants pleaded with the Supreme Spirit to shorten the time.

The Supreme Spirit, moved by their pleas, agreed to reduce the punishment to 50 years. This was a glimmer of hope for the people, but they knew they would still face many challenges.

The upper world was a magical realm filled with superpowers and mysterious creatures. Every type of power was stored in precious stones, which were essential to the life of the creatures. Guardians, powerful beings with unique abilities, protected the gate between the upper world and Earth.

Mr. Smith, a renowned senior detective , told Casper, "Most historians believe that in the other world, the God of Supreme Power was betrayed by the Goddess of Peace, who married a vampire. The stories are captivating, but they may not be entirely true."

"But is the story *true*?" Casper asked, his eyes wide with curiosity.

Mrs. Smith, replied, "I can't say for sure. But I can tell you that the truth is hidden deep within the shadows, waiting to be revealed. And when it is, the world will never be the same."

The withdrawal of the stakes was a major concern for the university. They were studying at Oxford, one of the most prestigious universities in the world.

Casper, determined to find **Ada**, went to the university, believing in his logistics that a princess would receive the best education in the whole world.

Three weeks later, the professor paired Casper and Claire for a project on Greek mythological characters. They were to portray *Eros and Psyche* in a play. As they worked on costumes, Casper asked Claire to tell him more about her past. She revealed that her mother had left when she was young, and she was raised by her father. After his death, Uncle Louis Harper took care of her in the U.S., but he never told her who her mother was. This sparked divine thoughts in Casper, and he began to wonder about Claire's true identity. They decided to find *costumes* the very next day.

"We're screwed," Claire groaned to Casper, "We didn't get the costumes."

"Don't panic," Casper replied with a wink. "I know just the place."

They stumbled upon a quaint, centuries-old shop called "**Lost and Found**." The shopkeeper, an old lady with eyes that seemed to see right through you, smiled knowingly. "The two dresses in the corner," she said, her voice barely a whisper.

"How did you know?" Casper asked, amazed.

"*I read your minds*," she replied, her smile widening.

While Casper chatted with the old lady, Claire was drawn to a shimmering *pearl* necklace.

"It's *beautiful*," she murmured, her fingers tracing the intricate design.

"It belonged to my great-great-great grandfather," the old lady said. "He bought it from a **wizard's carnival**."

"A wizard!! What?" Casper exclaimed, his eyes wide.

Claire's heart pounded. She knew it. The necklace belonged to her father, who had hidden it away as pearl necklace to keep it safe.

"What are you thinking?" Casper teased, nudging her arm.

"Nothing," Claire replied, her gaze fixed on the necklace.

They tried on the dresses and were stunned by their perfect fit. As they left the shop, Claire couldn't shake the feeling about the past with the necklace.

The next day, disaster struck. Casper was sick, and Edward, the school's heartthrob, had landed the lead role.

Claire was terrified. How could she possibly perform with a stranger?

But when Edward arrived, her fears were quickly replaced by a different kind of shock. Girls were swooning over him, their eyes sparkling with admiration.

Claire couldn't help but wonder, "What's so special about him?"

As the teacher called everyone to their positions, Claire took a deep breath and prepared to face the unknown.

"The final performance was just one day away after two days of practice."

"Edward!" Claire exclaimed *angrily*. "Why can't you take this seriously? The teacher said we need to get along and play the script!"

"*My lady*," Edward replied, "please pass me the script."

As the day of the show approached, Claire grew increasingly nervous about the kissing scene. During the performance, however, Edward surprised her by kissing her hand instead. This unexpected gesture made her feel more comfortable and relaxed.

"I'm sorry if I changed something," Edward apologised afterward. "I thought you might be nervous."

"No, it's fine," Claire assured him.

"Let's go *celebrate*," Edward said.

Casper, being jealous, watched the video of the play and became angry. He called Claire and told her he wanted to meet up that night. Claire declined, saying she had plans with Edward. This made Casper more *furious*.

At the restaurant named "The Perch", Claire asked Edward if he had any special talents.

"*I can read minds*," he revealed.

"I can read everyone's mind except yours. I guess you're the chosen one."

Claire was intrigued. "Tell me what that man over there is thinking about me."

"He thinks you're not wearing enough makeup," Edward replied. "And he's touching his phone a lot, weird!!. I have another power: *I can predict the future*. That man is going to slip on a banana peel."

Just as Edward predicted, a waiter slipped on a banana peel and fell.

"That's incredible," Claire said.

After dinner, as they walked through the city, Edward couldn't shake the feeling of unease. He had seen a vision of danger lurking for Claire.

"Claire," he said, stopping abruptly. "I need to tell you something."

Claire turned to face him, concern etched on her face. "What is it, Edward?"

"I had a premonition," he confessed. "I saw you getting into an accident if you took a cab home."

Claire's eyes widened. "Are you serious?"

"I'm sure of it," Edward replied. "Please, let me drive you home."

Claire hesitated, but she couldn't deny the weight of his words. She nodded, and they continued their journey, with a newfound sense of urgency. As they pulled up to her house, Claire thanked Edward for his concern.

"You might have just saved my life," she said, smiling gratefully.

"No, I just wanted to help," Edward said.

The next day, Claire met up with Casper. He was acting a little strange, his mood noticeably off.

'Why are you being so weird?' Claire asked, raising an eyebrow.

'I'm not weird,' Casper replied defensively.

'Wanna go to the carnival tonight? My truck's ready.'

Claire shrugged. 'Sure, why not? We're free anyway.'

The sun was beginning to set, casting long shadows across the carnival grounds. Casper and Claire, two best friends, were brimming with excitement as they wandered through the colourful stalls and rides.

The air was filled with the sweet aroma of cotton candy, the sound of laughter, and the distant music from the Ferris wheel.

"Look, Casper! They have a whole section dedicated to games of chance!" Claire exclaimed, her eyes sparkling with anticipation.

"I know, Claire! I wonder if we can win anything," Casper replied, his voice filled with confidence.

"Let's try that ring toss game. I'm sure I can win a *prize* for you," Casper suggested.

"*Okay*, but if you don't win, you have to buy me a cotton candy," Claire *bargained*.

"*Deal*," Casper agreed, grinning.

As they approached the ring toss game, the carnival host announced, "Ladies and gentlemen, step right up and test your *luck!* Win a prize and impress your friends!"

Casper picked up a ring and tossed it towards a bottle. The ring sailed through the air, but it missed the target by a hair.

"*Ha! I guess you owe me a cotton candy,*" Claire teased.

"Aw, man. But I'll buy you two cotton candies if you let me try again," Casper pleaded.

"Okay, but only if you buy me a giant stuffed animal too," Claire countered.

"*Deal*," Casper said, determined to win.

With renewed focus, Casper tossed the ring again. This time, it landed perfectly on the bottle.

"Yes! I won!" Casper cheered, his face lighting up with joy.

"Great! Now you have to buy me all three things," Claire replied, her eyes wide with excitement.

"Fine, but I'm getting my money back from the game first," Casper joked.

"Ha! You're so funny, Casper," Claire laughed.

As the sun dipped below the horizon, Casper and Claire continued their adventure, their laughter echoing through the carnival grounds. With their pockets full of prizes and their hearts full of joy, they knew it was a night they would never forget.

Meanwhile, the mystery of Ada continued to deepen. No one seemed to know anything about her.

As the semester began, the students were divided into groups for their projects. Claire, Luke, Jake, Erika, and Isabelle were assigned to one group, while Edward, Louie, Casper, Maria, and Clover were in another. The competition was fierce. The winning group would receive a prestigious trophy and national and international recognition.

Each student was *brilliant and unique,* but only one group could claim the top prize. The pressure was on."

"The competition was so intense that every student felt the pressure mounting. With only a week to go before the project presentations on November fifth,, everyone was working tirelessly to conduct their research.

Edward's team was focused on researching the *T-virus vaccine*, while Claire's group was exploring the creation of an **antidote H** that required a vampire's hair as a crucial ingredient. The challenge was that this rare element could only be found in the *underworld*, not on Earth.

If successful, their groundbreaking research would not only bring them recognition within their college but also worldwide acclaim. However, the question remained: where could they possibly obtain a vampire's hair?

Erika, ever the resourceful one, suggested visiting a mysterious shop called *'Lost and Found.'* Legend had it that the elderly woman who ran the shop possessed artefacts related to *witches, wizards, and other supernatural creatures.* Claire, determined to find the necessary ingredient for her research, decided to **investigate.**"

"They approached the old woman, her wrinkled face etched with wisdom. She spoke in hushed tones, her voice carrying a hint of urgency. 'A researcher has already taken the hair,' she revealed. 'He swore to secrecy, but his intentions are far from pure. I've seen into his mind... and his plans are sinister.'

She paused, her eyes fixed on the group. 'I won't reveal his identity, but I'll give you a clue:

He's known not by his true name, but by a fabricated one. He's like a snake, lurking in the shadows, ready to strike. And remember, he's as elusive as an owl, often seen in the dead of night.'

The old woman's words sent a chill down their spines. They knew they had a difficult task ahead.

Jack: "So, what do we do now?"
Erika: "We need to figure out who this researcher is."

Erika suggested, 'It could be Dr. Winston.'
Jack said, 'It could be Dr. James.'
Everyone had different guesses....

Claire said, "I think I have an idea. Remember what the old woman said? He's like a snake—charming on the outside, but dangerous within. And he's often seen at night. Who fits that description?". Definitely, that's "Dr. Roy?".

Erika questioned,,"You think it's him?"

Claire said,"I'm almost certain. He's always working late, and he's got that... certain something about him. You know, that kind of fake charm."

Jack interrupted, "Well, we can't just accuse him without proof."

Erika suggested, "We need to find a way to sneak into the research centre and see if he's there at night."

Claire commanded, "That's what we'll do."

With a newfound determination, they decided to investigate. Under the cover of darkness, they planned to sneak into the research centre and confront Dr. Roy. The fate of the stolen hair, and perhaps even their own safety, hung in the balance.

The plans were shrouded in secrecy, but Claire knew she couldn't face the task alone. Edward was the perfect accomplice. IIe would undoubtedly know the ins and outs of the lab and could help them navigate the treacherous terrain.

Claire approached Edward with her proposal, her heart pounding in her chest. To her relief, he agreed without hesitation. Their mission was clear: infiltrate the lab, retrieve the mysterious hair, and keep their identities hidden at all costs.

Late that night, under the cover of darkness, Claire and Edward made their way to the imposing structure of Dr. Roy's research lab. With a nervous glance at the security cameras, Edward slipped his pass through the scanner, granting them access.

The lab was a labyrinth of sterile corridors and dimly lit rooms. As they ventured deeper into the facility, their hearts raced with anticipation and a touch of fear. The air was thick with the scent of chemicals and scientific equipment, and the silence was broken only by the soft hum of machinery.

Suddenly, they heard a faint sound from down the hall. Dr. Roy was approaching! Panic surged through them as they darted into the nearest empty room, their breath catching in their throats.

Dr. Roy's footsteps echoed in the hallway as he passed by, unaware of their presence. Once the coast was clear, Claire and Edward emerged from their hiding place and resumed their search.

After what felt like hours of combing through the lab, Claire finally spotted it.

Nestled in a dusty, black wooden box with a worn leather cover was the hair they sought.

As she carefully opened the box, a wave of astonishment washed over her.

The hair seemed to shimmer with an otherworldly light, as if it were alive.

Edward, sensing her unease, asked, "Are you alright?" Claire nodded, her voice barely a whisper. "Just a little overwhelmed," she replied.

As they prepared to leave, disaster struck. A vial of **liquid** X slipped from Edward's grasp, shattering on the floor. The noxious liquid spread rapidly, threatening to leave a telltale trace of their intrusion. With no time to waste, they fled the lab, their hearts pounding in their chests.

Back at their homes, Claire carefully stowed the precious hair in a hidden compartment. The next day, as they worked on the H antidote project in the chemistry lab, a strange feeling washed over Claire. She felt a sudden urge to abandon the project, but Erika, their determined team mate, wouldn't hear of it.

With only two days left before the research paper deadline, the pressure was mounting. Edward's team had successfully created the T Virus vaccine, but the H antidote remained elusive. Despite their exhaustion, they pushed themselves to the limit, their determination unwavering.

Finally, after countless hours of experimentation, they achieved a breakthrough. The H antidote was complete! They knew the significance of their discovery and the potential danger it posed. They asked their teacher to keep the antidote a secret, fearing the consequences if it fell into the wrong hands.

Everyone agreed except Erika, who was consumed by a bitter jealousy. She couldn't bear to see Claire's success, and her envy threatened to tear the team apart.

Despite the internal conflict, they managed to submit the research paper on time. The results would be announced in a month, and the team eagerly awaited the outcome.

With the project behind them, they had a month of well-deserved freedom. Some planned to relax and recharge, while others sought out summer programs to expand their knowledge.

Claire, however, had a different mission in mind. She needed to return to her true form and complete the task she had been given. The ancient castle, located 150 miles away from the university, held the key to her transformation.

As she prepared to leave, Casper, questioned her destination. Claire remained silent, a mysterious glint in her eye. She knew that the journey ahead would be perilous, but she was determined to see it through to the end.

Casper's recruitment efforts had taken an unexpected turn; he found himself drawn to understanding who Claire truly was and what her intentions might be.

After leaving the university, he couldn't shake the feeling that something was off.
   A nagging instinct urged him to follow her.

When Claire caught sight of him trailing behind, she quickly changed direction, veering away from the abundant house and heading toward the research centre. There, she sought out Edward, determined to keep her plans hidden from Casper.

She couldn't afford to let him in on what she was really up to.

From a distance, Casper watched as Claire approached Edward, and a rush of anger surged through him.

"Why did she lie?" he muttered to himself, frustration bubbling over. The betrayal stung deeply, and in his anger, he turned on his heel and stormed away.

"Is everything alright?" Edward asked, noticing the tension in Claire's demean-or.

Claire forced a smile. "Yes, everything's fine. Just... a lot on my mind."

Once they left the centre together, Edward couldn't shake the feeling that something was wrong.

"You seem distracted. Is there something you want to tell me?"

Claire hesitated. "It's nothing. Just... something I need to take care of."

At precisely midnight, Claire summoned her courage and made her way to the abandoned house.

The air was thick with anticipation as she stepped inside, drawn to a haunting painting that adorned one of the walls.

It depicted a beautiful woman, a man, and a little girl, frozen in time.

In that moment, she felt a surge of energy and transformed into Ada —a striking figure with mesmerising blue eyes, a flowing red dress that danced with the shadows, and an antique locket around her neck that glimmered faintly in the dim light.

She radiated a captivating charm, one that would linger in the minds of anyone who crossed her path.

With purpose, Ada descended into the basement, where she found an ancient tree pulsating with a soft blue glow.

Its vibrant energy seemed to beckon her closer.

Gathering her thoughts, she whispered a powerful incantation:

'הָעוֹלָם שֶׁלִּי, הָעוֹלָם שֶׁלָּךְ אֱלֹהִי, גְּרֹם לְדֶלֶת הָעוֹלָם הָעֶלְיוֹן לְהִתְעוֹרֵר לַחַיִּים

ha'olam shli, ha'olam shlach elohi, gram
ledelet ha'olam ha'alion lehitorer lechi'im
"My world, your world divine,
Make the up-world door come to life"

As her words resonated through the space, a shimmering gate swung open, revealing a breathtaking celestial realm. It was a paradise filled with swans gliding gracefully across a sparkling lake, surrounded by lush greenery and an overwhelming sense of peace. Ada transformed once more, this time into a radiant princess with cascading blonde hair and striking green eyes, adorned in a gown that shimmered like starlight.

She felt like a fairy, enveloped in an aura of otherworldly beauty.

In this enchanted place, she found her mother waiting for her. "Ada! I was beginning to worry," her mother said, relief flooding her voice.

"I had to come. I learned something terrible about Dr. Roy," Ada replied, urgency in her tone.

"He's planning something catastrophic. I saw it in his mind."

Her mother's expression turned grave. "What is he planning?"

"He wants to create a rift between worlds, which could lead to chaos and destruction here," Ada explained, her voice trembling. "We have to stop him."

Her mother's gaze was intense. "Ada, you must remain steadfast on your path. If you alter the future even slightly, the consequences could be dire for the world."

Meanwhile, back in the real world, Casper felt a growing sense of urgency.

He dialled Mrs. Smith, recounting the troubling behaviour he had observed from Claire.

"Something isn't right with her," he admitted, frustration evident in his voice.

"Casper," Mrs. Smith replied, her tone steady, "it sounds like you're overwhelmed by your emotions. You need to focus on uncovering the hidden vampires.

I've discovered a way to expose them.

It's essential that you take precautions."

"What kind of *precautions*?" Casper asked, his heart racing.

"Keep an eye on them during sunny days. Their skin will shimmer under the sunlight, their eyes will change colour, and they will possess the unsettling ability to read minds," she instructed.

"Thanks, Mrs. Smith. I'll be careful," he promised, determination settling over him as he hung up the phone.

He needed to piece together the mysteries surrounding Claire and the vampires, but time was running out.

The weight of his mission pressed heavily on his shoulders, yet he felt a spark of hope. Whatever it took, he shall uncover the truth.

CHAPTER TWO

TRUTH

At the USC headquarters, we see Edward entering a dimly lit conference room for a meeting with Dr. John, the enigmatic head of the company. The air is thick with tension as they begin discussing the consequences of harbouring the alien.

"The alien's name is Bruno," Dr. John whispered, his eyes darting nervously around the room. "He's the son of the former king of Mars, seeking refuge on Earth."

Edward leaned in, his voice barely audible. "But what about the Shelds? They're after him, aren't they?"

Dr. John's face paled. "The Shelds... they're supernatural creatures with unimaginable powers. They can extend souls, infiltrate minds, teleport at will, and transform their very essence."

"They're too powerful to be controlled," Edward hissed, a bead of sweat trickling down his temple.

Dr. John reached into his pocket, producing a small, pulsating device.

"Don't worry. This secret gadget will help you navigate and mask your location. If the Shelds arrive..." His voice trailed off ominously.

"What then?" Edward pressed.

"We'll catch them with our most advanced technology. You'll find weapons in the car's back seat and behind the rearview mirror. Be prepared for anything."

Edward hesitated, then nodded grimly. "Yes, sir."

Meanwhile, at a decrepit thrift store across town, reality seemed to warp. Two men materialised out of thin air, their forms shimmering as they assumed the appearance of the bewildered shopkeeper. They now looked like bearded Indian men, but their eyes... their eyes held an otherworldly gleam.

Back at USC headquarters, Bruno arrived for a private meeting with the staff. His skin was a sickly green, his face bore an unsettling expression, and his eyes... Edward shuddered as Dr. John described them.

"Pink eyes?" Edward repeated, his voice quavering. "Sounds... creepy."

The scene shifted to a hotel, where the two disguised Shelds cornered the attendant.

"Where is he?" they demanded in unison, their voices an unnatural chorus.

"Who?" the attendant stammered.

"The one with the pink eyes," they hissed.

When the attendant claimed ignorance, the Shelds' eyes flashed. In an instant, they had invaded the poor man's mind, sifting through his neurones like data files. Finding nothing of value, they returned to their bodies, but not before draining the attendant of his life force. He collapsed, a withered husk.

Edward met with Bruno, hastily disguising him as a human. They couldn't change his telltale pink eyes, so they resorted to coloured contact lenses. As they sat in a crowded restaurant, Edward's hand never strayed far from his concealed weapon.

Bruno fidgeted with his new contact lenses. "How do humans see through these things? It's like looking through pond scum."

Edward stifled a laugh. "Just try not to blink too much. And remember, no tentacles at the dinner table."

"Tentacles?" Bruno looked offended. "I'll have you know, we Martians evolved beyond tentacles eons ago. We're more into psychic appendages now."

"Right," Edward nodded, trying to keep a straight face. "Just keep your psychic appendages to yourself, especially around the calamari."

As they perused the menu, Bruno's eyes widened. "Wait, you eat cow? On Mars, they're our intellectuals!"

Edward nearly choked on his water. "Well, here they're more of a... delicacy. Maybe stick to the salad?"

"Salad?" Bruno scoffed. "Oh yes, because nothing says 'blend in' like an alien prince eating lawn clippings."

Their banter was interrupted as the disguised Shelds burst into the restaurant, their gazes sweeping the room.

"Quick," Edward hissed, "act natural!"

Bruno immediately stiffened, his movements becoming robotic. "GREETINGS, FELLOW HUMAN. I AM ENJOYING THIS NORMAL EARTH MEAL WITH MY NORMAL HUMAN OESOPHAGUS."

Edward face-palmed. "I said act natural, not like you're auditioning for a B-movie!"

As they hurried to the car, Bruno tripped over his own feet. "How do you balance on just two legs? This is like trying to walk on chopsticks!"

"Less quipping, more running!" Edward grabbed Bruno's arm, dragging him along.

The true horror was just beginning, but Edward knew that even in the darkest times, a little humour could be a powerful weapon against despair.

The disguised Shelds burst into the restaurant, their gazes sweeping the room. "Where's the USC agent?" they demanded of a terrified waiter.

"We don't have any agents here," the waiter stammered. "We don't know any agents from USC."

The Shelds' eyes narrowed suspiciously. Edward, sensing danger, hurried Bruno to the car.

But it was too late.

A high-speed chase ensued, with Edward desperately reaching for the gun hidden behind the rearview mirror.

He fired at the pursuing Shelds, but the bullets passed harmlessly through their now fiery forms

In a blinding flash, Bruno was ripped from the car, his body slamming into a nearby building with a sickening crunch.

Edward fumbled for the navigation device, but froze as he saw Bruno's lifeless form, chest crushed by the impact.

The USC team arrived, unleashing a barrage of gunfire on the Shelds.

But their human disguises simply melted away, revealing their true, terrifying forms.

With a sound like reality tearing, the Shelds vanished, teleporting to another world.

Edward stood amidst the chaos, his mind reeling. As he later walked to the university, determined to unravel the mystery of the Shelds' power, a chilling realisation dawned on him. When he had briefly glimpsed into their minds, he saw not just immense power, but the ability to predict — and change — the future itself.

The true horror was just beginning.

At night, something was off with Casper. It was a full moon night with a red twist to it. It seemed familiar. Suddenly, something stirred in his mind. A black-suited woman with a baby lying in the bed. A light of fire came to the house, burning it. The baby was sent to the big eagle heading for the sky, but it was too late for the mother to come out of that packed house.

The suspense was about to be opened, but suddenly something went in from his window, smashing it with a letter from unknown.
It was written in it:
"Find out about the vampire. The lady that appears in your dream will find its way to you before it is too late. Get the girl from the above. And save her."

Conscious, he looked out of the window, convinced it was a mysteriously dressed, hooded man with a big white beard, running for his life from that unwanted creature, which was seen never before. It was like a glowing fire, structured like a human body. Casper went down the stairs to look for the man, but it was too late to be true.

They disappeared. It was midnight, and when he saw the sky, he said, "Something feels off about it. It's the same sky as it was in my dream."

He went to his room, took out the book, which seemed like an ancient book titled:
"Creatures of the Universe"
This was an old book from his ancestors, the book he studied about the shelds, which were creatures of undoubted powers.
"Now, what is this sheld thing? I had to find the vampires first?," said Casper.

At the University, everybody was talking about the night sky, which seemed unusual. Something was about to happen.

Casper talked about the sheld to Claire, knowing about the whole truth, she said to give her the book of the creatures of the universe to study about them. But her intentions were not right about that book.

They went to Casper's house.
There was already someone glaring at Claire when they entered the room, about to take her soul.

Claire, with a supernatural ability, gave that man a floating in the air and threw him out from the window. The man teleported.

Casper said, "How did you do that?"

Claire said, "We don't have much time for that."

When she opened the book, she realised that page 666 was missing from it.

Casper said, "Yeah. It's missing in that volume"

"It was written about calling *demonic* powers to the world, which can destroy humanity," said Claire.

This made her uneasy, but to search for the person who had taken it.

She asked Casper, "Who did it belong to?"

He said, "*My ancestors.*"

Claire said, "Whom did you take that from?" The old lady from the lost and found.

They went to the old lady, telling her about what had happened.

While the lady said, "I knew this would happen. And the protector will arrive soon here. Take the **golden pearl** necklace and save us from the entity."

The lady handed over the golden pearl necklace. When Claire touched the necklace, it changed her to her original form as Ada. The old lady told Ada about the **blue pearl** belonging to Edward. And they had to work on it together.

Ada and Casper went to Edward's place, where on the way, Casper had a talk about why she hid her true identity.

Ada said, "*I can't inform you about that now, but this is also not your true form right now. You are-,*" Casper was confused when she went silent.

They arrived at Edward's place, not knowing what they would be seeing there.

At Edward's place, they saw the sheld in the form of fire. Ada *spun* it in the sky and threw the sheld into the teleported world.

"Ada, how are you here?" Edward asked.

"We don't have much time for this," Ada replied.

"How do you know it's Ada?" Casper asked.

"Can we all stop talking?" Ada said. She gave the blue pearl to Edward and said, "This belongs to you."

Edward took the *blue pearl* and turned it into a *necklace.*

"What in the world is going on?" Casper asked.

In Edward's room, he found a bag lying on the corner with a picture peeking out. In that picture, they saw a family with a little girl.

"Where did you find it?" Ada asked Edward.

At the back, it was written, "I will find your way."
"It's the same lady from the dream I had," Casper said.

"I know who she is. Come with me," Ada said.

They went to the abandoned mansion, curious to see what Ada would find.

In the car, on their way to the mansion, they encountered a wizard who tried to stop them from entering.

"Who are these young people here?" the wizard asked.

"Get out of our way. It's urgent, wizard," Edward told him.

"No, it's not. I'm here to stop you," the wizard said, thunder lightning in the background.

The flying wizard landed on the ground and jerked the car.

"Ada! Are you alright?" Edward screamed.

"Yes, I am," Ada said.

They tripped out of the car and took the blue pearl necklace. As Edward wore it, his hairs turned blonde, his eyes turned red, and he used his powers to throw the wizard away from them.

The wizard cast a spell on Casper, causing him to be unable to move. Casper told Ada and Edward to leave him and go to the mansion as fast as they could. The wizard was unable to catch them.

They went to the mansion and were terrified when they saw the portal in the middle of the hall was open, and shields were coming out of it.

In the wizard's mind, Casper saw the past, where they learned that the shield could only be stopped by closing the portal.

Casper transferred this information to Edward and Ada through his psychic skills.

Ada knew what had to be done and told Edward she would go find the white stone before it was too late to stop more shelds from entering.

Edward started using his powers to close the portal and stop the shelds from entering, but his powers were too weak to close it.

While searching for the stone, Ada found a stick and saw that the white stone had a message written on it.

It said, "Whoever is absorbed must be sacrificed. If not, the portal won't close without the sacrifice of the witched, ugly head."

Ada began to solve the riddle when she connected it logically to the *ugly-faced wizard*. She realised that if she sent the wizard with the shelds, they could close the door.

The sacrifice would be fulfilled by the white stone, golden pearl, and blue pearl, which could merge their powers and close the door.

"Edward! Catch!" Ada screamed, tossing the shimmering white stone into the air.

She had combined it with *golden and blue pearl, and after mixing them all together, a shiny gold crystal was formed.* Ada handed it to Edward, her eyes wide with urgency. "You know what to do!"

Edward nodded, determination etched on his face. "We have to break the spell! Casper, get the wizard inside the house!"

With a grunt, Casper dragged the wizard into the dimly lit room.

As the portal began to spin faster and faster, the shields started to emerge.

It's expanding!" Casper shouted over the growing roar.

Ada's heart raced. "We need to close it! I have to cast the spell."

She grabbed the stone and pointed at the swirling portal. "Casper, drag the wizard in! I'll cast the spell! Oblique the deer, make the world free!"

"Right!" Casper replied, his voice filled with urgency.

He thrust the wizard toward the portal.

The wizard, with her hideous, twisted face, snarled as Ada threw the crystal into the portal.

"No! You can't do this!" she screeched.

"Close the portal!" Edward shouted, his voice cutting through the chaos. "Ada, what did you throw in?"

"The wizard!" Ada gasped, watching as the portal absorbed all the shelds from around the world.

The portal began to close, a dazzling display of blue, purple, and gold lightning erupted. "It's working!" Casper exclaimed, stepping back in awe.

Finally, the portal closed with a loud crack, leaving the room still once more. The three of them stood there, catching their breath.

But then they noticed the lady in the picture frame; her eyes had turned from blue to red.

"That can't be good," Edward muttered.

Ada, feeling dizzy, fainted. "Ada!" Edward worried, rushing to catch her as she collapsed. "Casper, help me!"

Casper hurried over. "We need to get her to safety." They managed to place her in the car, and as they drove, Casper said, "I need to rest. I'm heading to my friend's house."

Edward hesitated. "Are you sure that's a good idea? It doesn't feel right."

Casper shrugged, masking his intentions. "I'll be fine. You two take care of each other." He stepped out, leaving Edward with a sinking feeling in his gut.

As they drove home, the sky shimmered with an aurora-like pattern, painting the scene with ethereal colours. Edward glanced at Ada, who looked peaceful while asleep. A strand of hair fell over her face, and he gently tucked it behind her ear. Memories flooded back—times at the carnival, laughter, joy.

Ada stirred, her eyes fluttering open. "Edward?" she murmured, still groggy.

"Just rest, Ada. We're almost home," he replied softly.

When they arrived at her house, Edward carefully helped her through the window to her bedroom, then quietly left, the weight of the day settling heavily on him.

Meanwhile, Casper met with Mrs. Smith. "Claire is a vampire, but I don't think she's bad," he said, concern in his voice.

Mrs. Smith nodded. "My instincts say the same, but we must be cautious."

"Is there anyone else we should be worried about?" Casper asked, his brow furrowing.

"I think so. We need to keep our eyes open," she replied, glancing around nervously.

"What's up with Dr. Roy? He seems to be missing," Casper added, his frustration growing.

Mrs. Smith sighed. "I don't know. Stop making jokes, Casper."

"Umm... okay," he muttered, trying to hide his irritation.

The next day at the university, Ada, disguised as Claire, approached Edward. "What's up? You're acting weird today."

"It's been only five minutes since we met, Ada," Edward replied, a teasing smile on his face.

"My name is Claire. Be careful!" she warned, eyes wide.

"Okay, my lady," Edward chuckled, shaking his head.

As their biology class began, Casper leaned over to Ada. "Who are you? You seem... different today."

Ada widened her eyes and replied, "Not really. Just trying to keep it together."

"Right," he said, intrigued but skeptical.

As the lecture droned on, Ada's mind raced. The weight of her double life as Claire felt heavier each day. She caught Edward's gaze across the room, and a flutter of anxiety stirred in her stomach.

During a break, Casper pulled her aside, his expression serious. "Ada, are you sure everything's okay? You seem... off."

"I'm fine, Casper. Just tired," she replied, forcing a smile.

He studied her for a moment.

"Look, I know you're trying to protect us, but if there's something going on, you need to tell me. I can help."

Ada hesitated. Should she reveal her secret?

But the implications were too *risky*. "I promise, it's nothing I can't handle."

Casper frowned but didn't press further. "Just watch your back, okay?"

Meanwhile, Edward lingered near the door, feeling the tension. He approached Ada after Casper walked away. "You're really not okay, are you?"

She sighed, running a hand through her hair. "It's complicated, Edward. Just... trust me."

"Trust is a two-way street," he said gently, concern etched on his face.

Before she could respond, a loud crash echoed from the lab across the hall. Students rushed to see what happened.

Ada felt a surge of adrenaline.
Something told her this was connected to the growing unrest surrounding Claire.

As they approached the commotion, a figure stumbled out, panic in their eyes. It was Dr. Roy, disheveled and wild-eyed.

"Get back! You don't understand!" he shouted, his voice breaking.

"Dr. Roy?" Casper called out, stepping forward. "What happened?"

"They're coming!" he gasped, clutching his arm, which was bandaged and stained. "I couldn't stop them. You have to believe me!"

The room fell silent, everyone watching, apprehensive. Ada felt a chill crawl up her spine.

"Who's coming?" Edward asked, his brow furrowing.

Dr. Roy glanced around, then lowered his voice. "Vampires. They're not just myths anymore. They're gathering, and they want something from us."

Ada exchanged a glance with Casper, both of them realising the danger had just escalated.

"What do they want?" she asked, her heart racing.

"They're searching for something—something powerful. If they find it, no one will be safe," Dr. Roy warned.

Edward stepped closer to Ada, protective. "We need to figure out what this is about, and fast."

As Dr. Roy struggled to regain composure, Ada felt an urgent pull inside her.

The line between her worlds was blurring, and she needed to act before it unraveled completely.

"Meet me tonight," she whispered to Edward. "I think I know where we can find answers."

CHAPTER THREE

THE PAST RIVALRY

That evening, as dusk settled over the campus, Ada steeled herself. Beneath her human facade as Claire lay a secret she had guarded fiercely: she was a vampire princess, the last of her line, and the weight of her legacy was becoming unbearable.

In the old library, she found Edward waiting, worry etched on his face.

"You're late," he said, glancing around as if expecting trouble.

"I had to make sure I wasn't followed," she replied, her pulse quickening.

"Did you bring the files?"

He slid a folder toward her. "Dr. Roy's research. It's unsettling—there's more to this vampire threat than we thought."

Ada opened the folder and felt her breath catch. The documents detailed an ancient artefact, said to amplify a vampire's power. It was exactly what she feared—the very thing that could endanger her world and humanity's.

"Why do they want this?" she whispered, tracing an illustration of a pendant that mirrored one she'd seen in her past life.

Edward leaned in closer. "Whoever possesses it could control not just their kind but everyone. If the vampires unite under one leader..."

"They could wreak havoc," Ada finished, her mind racing. "We need to find it before they do."

"Where do we start?" Edward asked, determination flickering in his eyes.

"There's an old chapel on the outskirts of town," Ada recalled. "Claire heard rumours about it being a site of power, but I never thought it was connected to my past."

Edward's expression shifted to one of concern. "You're sure this isn't just a fragment of your former life? A trick of memory?"

"I have to trust what I remember," she insisted, feeling the weight of her dual existence. "It's part of who I am, and it might lead us to the truth."

They ventured into the night, the air heavy with unspoken tension. Shadows danced among the trees, and Ada could feel the remnants of her royal lineage tugging at her. They reached the chapel, its crumbling facade standing like a sentinel against the night sky.

Inside, the atmosphere thickened with a history she could almost touch. The altar loomed ahead, overgrown with vines, and at its centre lay the pendant—just as she remembered it from her past life.

Suddenly, a figure emerged from the darkness, cloaked and menacing, eyes glinting with an unnatural hunger.

"You've come to claim what is not yours," it hissed, revealing sharp, elongated fangs.

Edward stepped protectively in front of her. "Who are you?"

"I am a guardian of this realm," the figure spat. "And you have trespassed here. The artefact belongs to my master."

Ada felt a surge of power rising within her, a familiar strength she had long suppressed as Claire. "We're not here to take anything. We seek answers."

"Answers will cost you dearly," the figure replied, advancing. "Your presence here is an affront to my master.""I know who I am," Ada declared, her voice steadying. "I am Ada, the vampire princess. I've returned to reclaim my past and protect my people."

The figure paused, a flicker of recognition crossing its features. "Princess? You're supposed to be lost."

"Not lost—hidden," she said, her resolve hardening. "I will not allow the darkness to consume either my kind or humanity. If there's a threat, we must face it together."

A tense silence stretched between them.

The guardian's expression shifted, calculating. "You seek knowledge, but the truth can be a weapon. Will you wield it wisely?"

"Yes," Ada replied, determination blazing in her eyes. "Help me understand what's happening, and I'll stand against the gathering forces."

As the guardian weighed her words, Ada felt the past closing in, intertwining with the present.

She was more than just a human; she was a princess with a legacy to uphold. Whatever darkness was brewing, she was ready to confront it—alongside Edward, her most trusted ally.

"Then follow me," the figure finally said, stepping aside. "The path to the truth is fraught with danger, but it's one you must take if you wish to protect both your worlds."

They moved deeper into the chapel, Ada felt the threads of her identity weaving together, her resolve solidifying. The past rivalry would soon become a fight for unity, and she was prepared to reclaim not just her title, but her destiny.

As they ventured deeper into the chapel, the dim light illuminated ancient murals depicting battles between vampires and their enemies.

Ada's heart raced; each image stirred memories of a time long forgotten, when she wielded power and faced treachery.

The guardian led them to a hidden chamber, its walls lined with more relics from her past. In the center, a stone pedestal bore the pendant, pulsating with an ethereal glow. "This is the source of your power," the guardian explained. "But it can only be activated by one who carries the blood of the ancients."

"What does that mean?" Edward asked, eyeing the pendant warily.

"It means," the guardian replied, "that you must embrace your lineage, Ada.
You are the key to awakening its true potential."

Ada stepped forward, drawn to the pendant. She could feel its energy resonating with her very essence. "But what if I'm not ready?" she whispered, fear creeping in. "What if I can't control it?"

"Control comes with understanding," the guardian said, crossing their arms.

"You must learn what it means to be a princess in this age, not just in the past."

"I won't let this power corrupt me," she vowed, glancing back at Edward, whose presence anchored her.

"I will use it to unite our worlds, to fight against the threat gathering in the shadows."

The guardian nodded slowly, a trace of respect in their gaze. "Very well. To access the pendant's power, you must confront your past—face the choices you made, the mistakes that haunt you."

With a deep breath, Ada approached the pedestal. As her fingers brushed against the cold metal, visions surged through her: battles fought, alliances forged, betrayals that led to her exile. Each memory was a thread in the tapestry of her identity.

Suddenly, the chamber darkened, and the walls flickered with images of her former self—powerful, yet conflicted. She saw herself leading a legion of vampires, driven by fear and vengeance, a ruler who had sacrificed her humanity for strength.

"Those were not the actions of a true leader," the guardian's voice echoed in her mind.
"You must rise above them."

"Who am I now?" Ada whispered, grappling with the weight of her legacy.

"You are the bridge between two worlds," the guardian replied, their tone firm. "Embrace that, and the pendant will reveal its true power."

Taking a steadying breath, Ada closed her eyes, recalling the lessons of compassion and unity she had learned in her current life as Claire. She opened herself to the pendant's energy, allowing it to flow through her.

A brilliant light enveloped the chamber, and Ada felt the strength of her ancestors coursing through her veins. In that moment, she became both Ada and Claire—the vampire princess and the human protector.

The pendant flared, casting a warm glow that illuminated the shadows lurking in the corners. "Now you are ready," the guardian said, a hint of awe in their voice.

But just then, a chilling laugh echoed from the shadows. A figure stepped forward—tall, cloaked, and unmistakably sinister.

"So, the lost princess has found her way home," they sneered. "But this time, I will not let you escape."

Ada's heart pounded.

"Who are you?"

"The one who will ensure your reign ends before it begins," the figure said, revealing themselves as a vampire lord, ancient and powerful. "Your efforts to unite the clans will only lead to chaos. I will not allow it."

Edward stepped forward, fists clenched.

"We'll fight you."

The vampire lord laughed, a sound devoid of warmth.

"You think your resolve is enough? You underestimate the darkness that dwells within."

"I understand darkness well," Ada said, her voice steady. "But it's the light that will guide us through it."

With a wave of her hand, the pendant glowed brighter, casting the chamber in radiant light. Ada felt the power surge within her, ready to be unleashed.

"I won't let you threaten my people again."

The vampire lord snarled, eyes narrowing as shadows swirled around them.

"You may have awakened your past, but you have no idea the forces you're truly up against."

"Let's end this," she declared, drawing strength from the history that now fueled her purpose. The night was just beginning, and she would not stand alone.

The vampire lord's laughter echoed ominously, his shadowy form shifting as he drew closer.

"You speak of unity, yet the blood of betrayal runs deep in your veins. You are nothing without the very darkness you seek to reject."

"Enough!" Ada shouted, summoning the pendant's light to pierce through the gathering shadows.

"I won't let you manipulate me with fear or doubt. My power is not a weapon, but a shield."

With that declaration, the chamber transformed. The murals on the walls glowed vividly, depicting not just battles but moments of solidarity, alliances formed against the tide of darkness. The guardian watched with a knowing smile, sensing the tide turning.

The vampire lord, now visibly irked, surged forward, the shadows coiling around him like serpents.

"You think your memories will save you? I am the embodiment of your past mistakes. I am your father!"

The revelation struck like lightning. Ada staggered, emotions crashing over her —rage, confusion, betrayal.

"You... you're my father?"

"Yes, and I shall reclaim what is mine. You were always meant to be my weapon, Ada. This power should serve me, not you!"

"No!" Ada's voice rang with defiance.

"You abandoned me. You chose power over family, darkness over love. I will never follow in your footsteps."

Edward stepped closer, resolute.

"She is not a weapon, and neither are you. This is a choice she has made."

The vampire lord recoiled, caught between anger and a twisted sense of pride.

"You think you can change the nature of blood? You are bound to me!"

Ada raised the pendant high, its glow intensifying, enveloping the chamber in a brilliant light.

"I am not bound to your darkness. I choose my own path."

Drawing upon her memories of the past and the lessons of unity, Ada felt the energy of the pendant resonate with her purpose.

With a decisive motion, she unleashed a wave of light that shattered the shadows surrounding the vampire lord.

He stumbled back, snarling as the brilliance cut through the darkness, exposing the fragility of his ancient power. "You think you've won? I will not be so easily vanquished!"

"Perhaps," Ada replied, her voice steady.

"But I am no longer the girl who feared her heritage. I embrace all of who I am—both light and dark. And I will unite my people, regardless of your influence."

With renewed determination, Ada conjured a barrier of light around herself and Edward, protecting them from the vampire lord's onslaught.

"Together, we can forge a new legacy."

As the vampire lord unleashed his fury, shadows and light collided in a breathtaking display.

The very air crackled with energy as Ada and Edward stood firm, drawing strength from their bond.

"Fight alongside me," Ada urged, looking at Edward.

"We can end this together."

"I'm with you," he replied, his voice resolute.

They joined hands, channeling their combined power into the pendant.

The light swelled, forming a radiant vortex that pushed against the vampire lord's darkness.

"Foolish children!" he roared, desperation creeping into his voice.

"You cannot defeat what is eternal!"

But as Ada focused on the pendant, memories of love, sacrifice, and hope flooded her mind. The light intensified, enveloping the chamber, drowning out the shadows.

"Your time is over!" she shouted, pouring her heart into the energy.

The radiant force surged forward, breaking through the vampire lord's defences. In an explosion of light, he was consumed, his anguished scream echoing before silence enveloped the chamber.

Panting, Ada and Edward stood in the aftermath, the chamber aglow with the soft luminescence of the pendant.

"Is it... over?" Ada asked, disbelief mingling with relief.

The guardian stepped forward, a serene expression on their face.

"You have chosen your path, Ada. The darkness will always exist, but now you possess the strength to confront it."

"What do we do now?" Edward asked, glancing at Ada.

"We prepare for what comes next," Ada said, determination flooding her veins.

"There are still those who would seek to exploit our worlds. We must unite the clans and create a future where we can coexist."

As they turned to leave the chamber, the pendant's glow dimmed slightly, but its presence felt like a heartbeat—a reminder of the journey ahead.

Together, they stepped into the night, ready to face whatever challenges awaited them, united by the bonds of love, courage, and a shared purpose.

As the goddess of peace materialized in a radiant burst of light, the atmosphere shifted dramatically. The vampire lord's confidence wavered, yet his fury ignited a fierce determination.

"You dare confront me?" he spat, shadows swirling ominously around him. "I am the darkness that feeds on fear!"

The goddess, unwavering, stepped forward, her presence radiating a soothing warmth. "You mistake power for strength, and you have forgotten the true meaning of fear. It is not a weapon, but a prison of your own making."

With a flick of her wrist, she summoned a wave of light that surged toward the vampire lord.

He countered with a torrent of shadow, the two forces colliding in a violent explosion.

The ground trembled beneath them as energy crackled in the air, illuminating the chapel with flashes of brilliance and darkness.

"Your light cannot banish me!" he roared, unleashing a flurry of shadowy tendrils that lashed out like whips. They lashed at the goddess, but she danced gracefully, each movement a blend of elegance and strength.

As the tendrils struck, she absorbed their energy, transforming it into radiant bursts of light.

"You are fuelled by despair," she called out, but I draw strength from hope!"

Ada watched in awe as her mother wielded light with the precision of a master, countering each shadowy assault with waves of ethereal energy.

The chamber shimmered with their battle, each clash echoing with the weight of ages-old conflict.

The vampire lord, realising he could not overpower her directly, shifted tactics.

"You think your peace can hold me? I will shatter your ideals!" He conjured a vortex of darkness, a swirling tempest aimed directly at the goddess.

With a resolute stance, she raised her arms, channeling the energy of the pendant Ada held.

"Together, we will show you the power of unity!"

Ada felt the pendant resonate, a surge of energy coursing through her veins as she joined her mother's strength. She unleashed a beam of light that merged with the goddess's power, creating a dazzling explosion of illumination that pierced through the swirling shadows.

The vampire lord recoiled, his expression a mix of rage and fear.

"You cannot—!"

But the goddess pressed on, her voice steady and commanding.

"You have been blinded by your own ambition. Now, see what true strength looks like!"

In a moment of clarity, she focused her energy into a concentrated orb of light.

The shadows shuddered as she hurled it at the vampire lord, illuminating the entire chamber. The light engulfed him, breaking through the layers of darkness that clung to him.

"You will not escape your fate!" Ada cried, channeling her power alongside her mother's.

The vampire lord howled as the combined force of their energies collided with him, tearing through his defences. The shadows twisted and shrank, but he fought back, summoning the darkest parts of his being.

"Your light is weak! You will not defeat me!" he screamed, but the confidence in his voice faltered.

As the light intensified, the goddess stepped forward, her presence unwavering.

"It is not just my light, but the light of every soul that believes in peace."

With a final surge, she unleashed a blinding wave that consumed the vampire lord entirely.

In a flash of brilliance, the shadows dissipated, leaving only silence in their wake.

The air grew still, and Ada felt the weight of the moment. Together, they had confronted the darkness, and now it was banished.

Ada turned to her mother, heart pounding.

"Is it over?"

The goddess smiled softly, radiating warmth.

"For now, yes. But remember, true peace requires constant vigilance. The darkness may always return, but together, you and I will face it."

Ada nodded, feeling a sense of purpose ignite within her. They had not only defeated a powerful foe; they had forged an unbreakable bond. But this was not the *end*.

After the battle, Ada and Edward hurried to his car, the night air thick with tension and uncertainty.

As they drove away, her mind raced with fragmented thoughts of what had just transpired.

The weight of her mother's absence pressed heavily on her heart, and she struggled to process everything.

"Hey," Edward said gently, glancing at her.

"You're safe now."

His voice wrapped around her like a warm blanket, but fatigue overtook her.

The last thing she remembered was the soft hum of the engine and Edward's reassuring presence beside her. Darkness pulled her under, and she slipped into unconsciousness.

She nodded, feeling a flicker of hope ignite within her. Ada opened the window wider, the fresh morning air filling her lungs and pushing away the remnants of the previous night.

Her gaze caught on Edward, standing just outside her window, his expression a mix of concern and relief. He looked as if he hadn't moved all night, watching over her.

"Do you want to come in?" she asked, stepping back to make space.

"Edward?" she murmured, still groggy.

"Hey," he replied softly, stepping closer.

"You scared me. I didn't want to leave."

Ada felt a rush of gratitude and warmth at his dedication. "I'm sorry... I didn't mean to worry you."

"It's okay. You went through a lot," he said, his tone gentle. "I'm just glad you're awake."

They stood there in silence for a moment, the weight of the previous night's events lingering in the air. Ada felt a surge of emotions—relief, gratitude, and something deeper that she struggled to name.

"Thank you for being here," she finally said, her voice steadying. "I don't know what I would have done without you."

Edward met her gaze, his eyes searching hers.

"You're stronger than you realize, Ada. But I'll always be here to help you."

He hesitated for a moment, then nodded and stepped inside, the morning light illuminating his features.

"How are you feeling?" he asked, concern etched on his face.

"A bit overwhelmed," she admitted, moving to sit on the edge of her bed.

"It's just... everything happened so fast."

"I get that," he said, taking a seat beside her.

"But you faced it head-on. Not many could do what you did."

His words warmed her heart.

"I couldn't have done it without you. You were there when I needed you."

Silence stretched between them, heavy with unspoken thoughts and emotions. Ada looked down at her hands, feeling a mixture of vulnerability and strength.

"What do we do now?" she asked finally, breaking the tension.

Edward leaned forward, his expression serious.

"We figure it out together. Your mother mentioned vigilance. We need to stay alert—there's no telling if the darkness will return."

"Right," she replied, her resolve strengthening. "We need to be prepared."

"Let's start by talking about what we faced," Edward suggested.

"I think we need to understand it better."

Ada nodded, recalling the chaos, the shadows, the moment she felt her mother's presence fade.

"I felt so powerless, but then... I found strength. I realized I could fight back."

"That's huge," he said, a spark of admiration in his eyes. "You're not just a bystander in this. You have the power to confront it."

She took a deep breath, feeling the weight of his words settle in.

"But what if I can't do it again? What if it comes back stronger?"

"Then we'll face it together," he replied firmly.

"You don't have to do this alone."

His words resonated deeply, and for the first time since the battle, Ada felt a flicker of confidence.

"Okay. Together."

As they spoke, a plan began to form in her mind. They could train, learn more about what they were up against, and prepare for whatever might come next."We should research," she suggested.

"Find out more about the darkness and how to combat it."

Edward smiled, his eyes brightening. "I love that idea. I'll help you with anything you need."

With newfound determination, Ada began to map out a strategy.

The darkness may have been banished for now, but they would be ready if it dared to return.

"Let's start with the library," she said, excitement bubbling within her. "There might be old texts or anything that can help us understand."

"I'll drive," Edward offered, standing up and stretching. "Let's get to work." They prepared to leave, Ada felt a surge of hope.

They made their way to the grand library at University, its towering shelves lined with countless volumes, each holding untold secrets.

The scent of old books mixed with the faint aroma of coffee from a nearby café, creating a familiar and comforting atmosphere.

"This place always feels like it's alive with stories," Ada said, taking a deep breath as they entered.

Edward nodded, glancing around.

"It's the perfect spot to dig into the past.

Let's find something about the darkness."

They headed to the rare manuscripts section, a treasure trove of ancient texts. As they sifted through the dusty tomes, Ada felt a thrill of anticipation.

She pulled out a heavy, leather-bound book with intricate gold lettering.

"Here's something—'The Chronicles of Shadows.' It looks promising!" she exclaimed.

Edward leaned in, his eyes widening.

"Let's see what it says."

As they settled into a nearby study table, the atmosphere around them shifted from casual study to focused intensity. Ada flipped through the pages, revealing tales of ancient beings, battles fought in the realm of shadows, and the delicate balance between light and darkness.

"This account mentions a key artifact—a relic that could seal away dark forces," she said, excitement coursing through her.

"We need to find out where it is."

Edward's expression turned serious.

"If it's real, it could be our best defense. Let's search for any leads in the footnotes."

They worked diligently, their minds racing with possibilities.

Hours passed, but neither of them noticed the time slipping away.

The library grew quieter, the only sounds being the rustle of pages and their whispered discussions.

"I think I found something," Ada said suddenly, her finger tracing a line on the page.

"It mentions a hidden chamber beneath the university, where the relic might be kept."

Edward's eyes sparkled with intrigue.

"We have to investigate. This could be our chance to find it."

Ada felt a surge of adrenaline.

"Let's plan our next steps. We'll need to gather supplies and figure out how to access the chamber."

As they closed the book, the weight of their discovery settled around them. They weren't just preparing for a potential threat; they were embarking on an adventure that could change everything.

"Together," Edward said, a smile breaking across his face.

"Together," Ada echoed, her heart filled with newfound determination. The darkness may have returned, but so had their hope.

They spent the next few hours poring over the dusty tomes in the library, mapping out the university's layout.

The mention of the hidden chamber had sparked a flame in their minds, and they scoured every reference to secret passages and forgotten corridors.

"We'll need tools," Ada said, jotting down a list. "Flashlights, climbing gear, maybe even some ropes in case we encounter a drop."

Edward nodded, his expression serious.

"And we should check the historical archives.

There might be blueprints of the old buildings that could lead us to the entrance."

As the sun began to set, casting long shadows across the room, they finalized their plan.

"Meet me here tomorrow at dawn," Ada said, determination in her voice.

"We'll have everything ready."

"Dawn it is," Edward replied, his enthusiasm palpable. "This feels like the beginning of something big."

That night, Ada could hardly sleep. Her mind raced with possibilities: what secrets lay hidden beneath the university?

What challenges awaited them? Each thought fueled her resolve.

The next morning, they reconvened, their backpacks filled with gear and their spirits high.

"Let's do this," Edward said, and they set off towards the oldest part of the campus, where legends of the chamber lingered like whispers.

As they approached the crumbling stone wall that marked the boundary of the oldest buildings, Ada felt a shiver of anticipation.

"This is it," she said, glancing at Edward, who nodded, his eyes scanning for any signs of an entrance.

They searched methodically, tracing their fingers along the stones, looking for any irregularities. Then, just as they were about to lose hope, Ada's hand brushed against a loose stone.

"Here!" she exclaimed, pulling it away to reveal a narrow passageway.

Edward grinned, his excitement infectious.

"Let's go!"

With flashlights in hand, they squeezed into the darkness. The air was cool and musty, filled with the scent of damp earth. As they ventured deeper, the tunnel opened up, revealing a larger chamber illuminated by flickering beams of light.

"What is this place?" Ada whispered, awestruck by the ancient carvings that adorned the walls.

Symbols of forgotten lore and myth encircled them.

"I don't know, but it looks like we're on the right track," Edward replied, his voice echoing in the vastness.

Suddenly, a low rumble reverberated through the chamber. Ada's heart raced.

"What was that?"

"Maybe the relic is nearby," Edward suggested, moving toward a set of large stone doors at the far end of the room, intricately engraved and partially ajar.

"Be careful," Ada warned, her instincts kicking in. They both stepped closer, curiosity battling caution.

As they pushed the doors open, a rush of cold air enveloped them, and they stepped into a dimly lit hall that seemed to stretch endlessly. At its center stood an ornate pedestal, and on it rested an object wrapped in layers of dust—a relic shrouded in mystery.

"I can't believe we found it," Ada breathed, her eyes wide with wonder.

"But why does it feel... wrong?"

Edward's expression darkened. "Because sometimes the things we seek come with a price."

They approached the pedestal cautiously, the air thick with tension. As Ada reached out to brush away the dust, a strange energy pulsed from the relic, sending a shiver down her spine.

"What do you think it is?" she asked, her voice barely above a whisper.

"I don't know, but it feels powerful," Edward replied, studying the intricate patterns on the surface.

"We should be careful."

As Ada wiped away the last layer of dust, the relic emerged—a small, crystalline orb that shimmered with a light of its own. The moment it was fully revealed, the chamber trembled, and the carvings on the walls seemed to shift, as if awakening from a long slumber.

Suddenly, the doors they had entered through slammed shut with a thunderous boom, plunging them into semi-darkness. "What just happened?" Ada shouted, panic rising in her chest.

"We have to get out of here!" Edward exclaimed, scanning for another exit.

The chamber was now illuminated by the orb's glow, casting eerie shadows that danced along the walls. As they backed away from the pedestal, the ground beneath them began to tremble, and a low growl echoed from the depths of the darkness.

"What was that?" Ada asked, her heart racing.

"Whatever this is, it's guarding the relic," Edward said, his eyes wide with fear.

"We need to move!"

They turned and rushed toward the heavy doors, but they wouldn't budge.

"It's stuck!" Ada yelled, panic overtaking her.

Just then, the growling grew louder, and from the shadows emerged a figure—a massive creature cloaked in darkness, its eyes glowing with an unnatural light.

"Run!" Edward shouted, and they sprinted back into the chamber, desperately searching for a way out.

"Over there!" Ada pointed to a narrow passageway they hadn't noticed before, partially obscured by rubble.

They dashed toward it, the creature's snarls echoing in their ears.

As they slipped through the opening, the walls scraped against their shoulders, and they tumbled into a smaller tunnel that twisted and turned deeper into the earth.

"We can't stop!" Edward urged, adrenaline driving them forward.

The passageway opened into another chamber, this one filled with ancient artefacts and relics, their surfaces glinting in the orb's light.

"What is all this?" Ada asked, bewildered.

"Maybe it's a storage area," Edward replied, scanning the room. "But we can't stay here. That thing will find us."

As they moved cautiously through the room, Ada spotted a strange mural on the far wall. It depicted a figure holding the orb, surrounded by light, with shadowy forms lurking just outside the glow.

"This must be a warning," she said, her voice trembling.

"We need to find a way out," Edward insisted, examining the walls for any sign of an exit.

"If we can reach the surface, we can figure out what to do next."

Suddenly, a glimmer caught Ada's eye. It was another passage, hidden behind a pile of broken statues.

"Over here!" she called, and they hurried toward it.

As they squeezed through, the growling intensified behind them. They could feel the creature drawing closer.

"Faster!"

Edward urged, pushing through the narrow space.

They emerged into a dimly lit corridor, the air cooler and heavier.

"Do you hear that?" Ada asked, pausing to listen.

The growling was fading, but so was the orb's light, dimming as if its energy was waning.

"We need to keep moving before it comes back," Edward said, glancing nervously over his shoulder.

They hurried down the corridor, which seemed to stretch endlessly.

Just as they began to lose hope, they spotted a faint light ahead.

"That must be an exit!" Ada exclaimed, her heart racing.

As they approached, the light grew brighter, illuminating a set of wooden doors. With a final surge of energy, they flung the doors open and stumbled outside into the cool night air.

Gasping for breath, they found themselves in an overgrown courtyard, surrounded by towering trees and the ruins of ancient structures.

"We made it," Ada said, collapsing onto the ground.

Edward sat beside her, his expression a mix of relief and disbelief.

"But what now? We still have the relic, and whatever that creature is..."

"We need to figure out what we unleashed," Ada said, her mind racing.

"We can't just leave it like this. We have to understand its power and find a way to contain it."

Edward nodded, determination flickering in his eyes. "Together," he affirmed.

As they caught their breath, Ada and Edward exchanged ideas about the relic and its implications. The courtyard, though serene, felt charged with the weight of their discovery.

"First, we need to understand what that creature was," Edward said, standing up and brushing off dirt.

"The mural suggested it's a guardian, but a guardian of what?"

Ada pulled out her notebook, filled with sketches and notes. "The legends speak of the orb as a source of immense power—one that can either protect or destroy. That's why it was hidden beneath the university. Someone must have sealed it away for a reason."

"Let's retrace our steps," Edward suggested, "and gather more information from the archives. There must be more written about this place and its history."

They made their way back through the university grounds, determined to piece together the relic's past. In the archives, they uncovered a collection of old manuscripts detailing the university's foundation—a secret society known as the Keepers had once protected the relic, believing it contained the essence of ancient knowledge.

"The Keepers were dedicated to safeguarding powerful artefacts," Ada noted, her eyes scanning the texts. "This suggests that the orb was meant to be protected from misuse."

"And it explains why the chamber was hidden," Edward added, his fingers tracing over a faded map that indicated the locations of other hidden chambers throughout the campus.

"There could be more relics out there."

As they delved deeper, they stumbled upon references to rituals performed by the Keepers.

"These rituals were meant to strengthen the barrier between our world and whatever lies beyond," Ada said, her excitement building.

"We might be able to perform one to protect ourselves and the relic."

Edward's brows furrowed.

"But we'll need to gather the right ingredients—some of which might be hard to find. We should also prepare for the possibility that the creature could return."

The thought hung heavy in the air. With a plan forming, they spent the following days collecting materials, consulting with professors knowledgeable about ancient traditions, and exploring the depths of the university's archives.

In their research, they uncovered a list of ancient texts scattered throughout various libraries and museums, each tied to the Keepers and their practices. One particular text hinted at a "counter-ritual" that could bind the relic's power, preventing the creature from breaking free.

"It's risky," Ada warned, glancing at Edward as they reviewed the text.

"We'll have to perform this at the site of the relic. If we do it incorrectly, we could unleash more chaos."

"Then we'll just have to be careful," Edward replied, a steely determination in his eyes.

"This is our best chance to contain the darkness."

With their goal set, they organized one final expedition back to the chamber. Armed with the necessary materials and their notes, they felt a mix of excitement and dread. As they descended into the darkness again, the air felt different—charged, as if the relic awaited them.

Upon entering the chamber, the orb pulsed with an ethereal glow. They set up the items according to the instructions in the text, their hearts racing with each movement.

"Are you ready?" Edward asked, glancing at Ada.

"Ready as I'll ever be," she replied, her voice steady despite the anxiety bubbling beneath the surface.

They began the ritual, their voices echoing as they chanted the ancient incantations.

The orb responded, its light intensifying, filling the chamber with a radiant glow. Suddenly, the ground shook violently, and the creature's growl reverberated through the walls, echoing their fears.

"Keep going!" Ada urged, her eyes fixed on the orb as it vibrated in response to their words.

With a final shout, they completed the incantation. The light from the orb enveloped them, and a wave of energy surged through the chamber.

The creature's growling grew frantic, and then, with a final roar, it was silenced, drawn back into the shadows. The chamber fell still, the glow of the orb now steady and serene.

"Did it work?" Edward panted, still catching his breath.

Ada approached the pedestal, heart pounding as she examined the relic. "I think so. It's calm now. We've contained it."

As they stood together, the weight of their journey settled around them. They had uncovered mysteries long buried and confronted a darkness that threatened to break free. But their adventure was far from over.

"There's still so much we don't know," Ada said, looking back at the intricate carvings on the walls. "What other secrets are hidden beneath the university? What else did the Keepers protect?"

Edward nodded, a spark of curiosity igniting in his eyes.

"I guess we'll just have to find out. Together."

With that, they exited the chamber, leaving behind the relic —but taking with them a renewed sense of purpose. The shadows of shelds might always linger.

CHAPTER FOUR

THE AUTUMN FALL

The season of autumn enveloped the campus in a cascade of vibrant colours, signalling change and reflection. Claire, having transformed from her ethereal self into her human form, walked alongside her team—

—Luke, Jake, Erika, and Isabell—as they approached the university. Today was significant: the results of the competition were to be announced.

As they entered the auditorium, the atmosphere buzzed with anticipation. The stage was adorned with banners celebrating creativity and innovation.

Faculty members chatted excitedly, and students exchanged nervous glances.

"Are you ready for this?" Luke asked, adjusting his tie.

"I think so. Just remember to breathe," Claire replied, trying to quell her own nerves.

As the ceremony began, the head of the department stepped up to the podium, a warm smile on her face.

"Welcome, everyone! Thank you for joining us today to celebrate the incredible talent we've seen in this year's competition. Each team has put in remarkable effort, and I'm proud of you all."

The crowd erupted in applause, and Claire felt her heart race. The head teacher continued, "Now, without further ado, let's get to the results.

First, I'd like to announce the winners of the first prize."

Claire squeezed Jake's hand.

"This is it!"

"And the first prize goes to... Claire's Team!" The teacher's voice rang out, and the room erupted in cheers.

"We did it!" Claire shouted, hugging her teammates tightly.

"This is unreal!" Isabell exclaimed, jumping up and down. "All those late nights paid off!"

As the applause continued, Claire felt a rush of pride when her name was called for the merit prize.

She stood frozen for a moment before Erika nudged her forward.

"Go on, Claire! You deserve it!" she urged, beaming.

With a deep breath, Claire stepped up to the podium. "Thank you so much! I couldn't have done it without all of you."

As she accepted her award, she spotted Edward in the crowd, beaming with pride. He made his way over as the applause subsided. "Congratulations, Claire! You were incredible!"

"Thanks, Edward! I still can't believe we won!" she replied, her eyes sparkling.

"Let's celebrate! You owe me a treat for all this," he said with a playful grin.

"I will! Just give me a moment; I want to celebrate with the team first," she said, glancing back at her teammates, who were still reveling in their victory.

However, from the corner of the room, Ericka watched with a scowl. Her frustration boiled over as she whispered to herself, "How did Claire get the merit prize too? It's not fair." Unable to contain her feelings, she turned on her heel and left the event, her jealousy evident.

After the ceremony, the atmosphere was electric. Claire rejoined her team, who were buzzing with excitement.

"I can't believe we pulled it off!" Luke laughed, still holding his trophy.

"Let's get some food to celebrate!" Jake suggested, his eyes glinting with enthusiasm.

Claire nodded, her heart swelling with gratitude. "Absolutely! You guys are the best team I could ask for."

As they headed out, Edward lingered for a moment. "I'll catch up with you guys later. I just want to talk to Claire for a second."

Once they were alone, he said, "Seriously, you did amazing today. You deserve every bit of that recognition."

"Thanks, Edward. It means a lot coming from you," Claire replied, feeling a warmth spread through her.

"Just don't forget about that treat!" he said with a wink before rejoining the others.

After Edward left, Claire and her team decided to head to a nearby restaurant called "Bella's Bistro", a cozy spot known for its warm ambiance and delicious Italian food. As they entered, the comforting aroma of garlic and fresh herbs greeted them, making Claire's stomach rumble.

They settled into a large booth, the soft glow of pendant lights creating an inviting atmosphere.

"I can't believe we actually won!" Isabell exclaimed, her eyes shining with excitement.

"Right? All that hard work paid off!" Luke replied, leaning back with a satisfied grin. "We make a great team."

Claire raised her glass of sparkling water. "To teamwork and friendship! We couldn't have done it without each other."

"To us!" everyone cheered, clinking their glasses together.As they dug into their meals, laughter filled the air.

They shared stories about the competition, reminiscing about late-night brainstorming sessions and the moments that made them anxious.

"Remember when Jake almost set the project on fire?" Erika teased, smirking.

Jake laughed, shaking his head. "Hey, it was just a small flame! I thought we needed more 'passion' in our presentation."

"Passion? More like panic!" Luke shot back, and they all erupted in laughter.

Claire wiped a tear of laughter from her eye. "I thought we were going to lose it when you started waving that fire extinguisher around!"

"Yeah, I didn't realize it was a safety drill!" Jake said, grinning.

As they enjoyed their meals, Claire couldn't shake a strange feeling, as if someone were watching them.

Meanwhile, outside, a figure stood hidden in the shadows, observing the group intently.

"Okay, Claire, what's next for you?" Luke asked, breaking into her thoughts. "Any big plans after this?"

Claire hesitated, a mix of excitement and uncertainty washing over her.

"I'm not sure yet. I think I want to explore more projects—maybe even look into internships."

"That sounds awesome!" Isabell encouraged. "You'll definitely land something great."

Just then, Erika chimed in, "As long as you promise to take us all with you when you're famous!"

"Deal! I'll be the world's greatest intern," Claire laughed, but the unease lingered.

Outside, the figure moved closer, pulling out a phone and glancing down at it.

"They're here. I've got eyes on them," they whispered into the device, their voice low and urgent.

Back inside the bistro, Claire was oblivious to the looming presence. "I just hope we can stick together, no matter what happens next," she said, her gaze shifting to her friends.

"Of course! We're in this together," Erika affirmed, raising her fork for emphasis.

"Always," Luke echoed, a smile on his face.

The team continued their celebration, unaware of the tension building just outside. The figure stepped back into the shadows, watching as the waiter approached their table.

"Can I get you anything else?" the waiter asked.

"Just the check, please," Claire replied.

As they wrapped up their meal, Claire felt a slight chill run down her spine as the door swung open, sending a draft through the restaurant.

"Did you guys feel that?" Claire asked, glancing around.

"Just the autumn air," Jake said, brushing it off. "Nothing to worry about."

"Yeah, it's probably just the wind," Isabell added, but Claire's unease persisted.

As the night wore on, Luke suggested, "Let's take a group picture to remember this night!"

"Great idea!" Claire agreed, her smile brightening.

They huddled together, arms around each other, posing with wide grins. Just as the picture was snapped, a shadow flickered outside the window. The figure watched, their expression hardening.

"Okay, let's head out," Erika said, glancing at her watch. "I can't believe it's already late!"

"Let's walk by the lake! It's so pretty at night," Isabell suggested, excitement in her voice.

"Good call!" Claire replied, feeling a mix of anticipation and dread.

As they left the bistro, the figure melted into the darkness, following them at a distance. The group walked down the tree-lined street, the vibrant autumn leaves crunching underfoot.

"Look at those stars!" Jake said, pointing up. "It's like the sky is celebrating with us."

"Perfect night for a victory walk," Luke agreed. "We should make this a tradition."

"Definitely! And next time, I'm bringing dessert!" Isabell chimed in, her enthusiasm infectious.

But as they chatted and laughed, Claire's instincts tingled, and she glanced over her shoulder, feeling a presence behind them.

"Do you guys ever feel like someone's watching us?" she asked, trying to shake off the feeling.

"Nah, it's just your imagination," Erika replied with a chuckle.

"Yeah, it's a festive night! Nothing but good vibes," Luke added.

Still, Claire couldn't shake the feeling that they weren't alone. The cozy atmosphere of their celebration felt suddenly constricting, as if the shadows were closing in around them. Little did they know, danger lurked just behind them.

Suddenly, Edward pushed the figure away from Claire, adrenaline coursing through him. "Get away from her!" he shouted, fists ready.

The figure snarled, but before it could react, Edward tackled it. They exchanged blows, but in an instant, the figure vanished.

Breathing heavily, Edward turned to Claire. "We need to go. Now."

"What was that?" Claire asked, eyes wide with confusion.

"I don't know, but it's not safe here," he replied urgently. "We can't stay."

"Wait, what about the others?" Claire glanced around, panic rising.

"They'll be fine. Right now, we need to focus on getting out of here," Edward insisted, grabbing her arm. "Come on!"

Claire hesitated, fear creeping in. "What if it comes back?"

Edward met her gaze, resolve strong. "Then we'll be ready. Just trust me."

Edward pulled Claire into a run, urgency propelling them forward. "We can't stop now," he said, glancing back at the empty street.

"What was that thing?" Claire asked, breathless.

"I don't know, but we need to reach the warehouse. It's safer there," he replied.

They rounded a corner, shadows stretching around them. Claire hesitated. "What if it comes back?"

Edward stopped, meeting her gaze. "We'll be ready. Together."

After their harrowing escape, Edward and Claire found solace in each other's presence.

They spent hours together, sharing stories, laughter, and unspoken dreams. One evening, as they walked through the park, the stars twinkling above, Claire smiled softly.

"I never thought I'd feel safe again," she admitted, glancing at him.

Edward paused, meeting her gaze. "You're safe now. I'll always make sure of it."

Their eyes locked, and in that moment, something shifted. They leaned closer, and their lips brushed in a tentative kiss that blossomed into something deeper.

From that night on, they were inseparable, their bond growing stronger.

However, not everyone was thrilled about their relationship. Casper, Claire's friend, watched from the sidelines, harbouring a crush on her that made him increasingly protective.

One evening at a local bar, he confronted Edward.

"You really think she's good for you?" Casper asked, his tone skeptical as he leaned against the bar.

"What do you mean?" Edward replied, furrowing his brow.

"I just... I don't trust her with you," Casper shrugged, trying to mask his true feelings.

"Trust her? She's been through a lot, and she deserves someone who cares," Edward shot back, his frustration simmering.

Casper pressed on, "You think she's ready for a relationship after everything? She might just be using you to feel safe."

Ericka, who had a crush on Edward, joined in, sensing an opportunity to sway things her way.

"You need someone who can keep you grounded, Edward. Someone who isn't tangled up in this chaos."

Edward felt a surge of anger. "Are you serious? You don't even know her! Claire is brave and strong. She's exactly what I need."

Casper smirked, dismissing Edward's passion. "Brave? Or reckless? There's a difference."

"Maybe you're just jealous," Edward retorted, his patience wearing thin. "She makes me happy, and that's all that matters."

The tension hung thick in the air, but Edward's determination only grew. He knew Claire was worth fighting for.

Meanwhile, Mr. Smith and Louis Harper were reconnecting over coffee at a cozy café. It had been years since they last saw each other, and the joy of reunion filled the atmosphere.

"Can you believe it's been a decade?" Smith chuckled, shaking his head. "Feels like yesterday we were arguing about budgets."

Louis laughed heartily. "And you always won! But seriously, it's great to see you. We should keep in touch more often."

"Definitely," Smith replied, the warmth of friendship evident in his voice. "Let's not let work get in the way next time. Life's too short."

As Edward navigated his relationship with Claire, Dr. John, his boss, called him into his office one afternoon. The atmosphere was serious, and Edward felt a knot in his stomach.

"Edward," Dr. John began, leaning back in his chair, "I've been thinking. It might be time for you to leave the company."

Edward's heart raced. "What? Why?"

"You've given so much to this place. You deserve to enjoy your life, to explore other passions," Dr. John explained, his expression kind yet firm.

"Are you sure? I've worked here for so long," Edward replied, uncertainty creeping in.

"Absolutely. You've earned it. Life is too short to be tied down by work. Follow your heart," Dr. John encouraged, a smile breaking through his serious demeanour.

With that conversation weighing on his mind, Edward found himself at Claire's apartment later that evening.

He paced back and forth, trying to find the right words. When Claire walked in, she sensed his tension.

"What's wrong?" she asked, concern etched on her face.

"I just had a meeting with Dr. John," he said, stopping to face her.

"And?" Claire urged, leaning against the kitchen counter.

"He wants me to leave the company. He thinks I should enjoy life," Edward explained, his voice heavy with uncertainty.

Claire's eyes widened. "That sounds amazing! Why do you look so stressed?"

"I don't know. It's just... I've been here so long. What if I'm making the wrong choice?" he confessed, running a hand through his hair.

Claire stepped closer, placing a hand on his arm. "Edward, you deserve to be happy. You've been through so much. Don't let fear hold you back."

"Are you sure you'll support me if I do this?" he asked, searching her eyes for reassurance.

"Of course! I want you to follow your dreams, whatever they may be. I'm with you, no matter what," Claire reassured him, her sincerity shining through.

Edward felt a weight lift as her words sank in. "Okay, then I'll do it. I'll take the leap."

Just as the tension began to dissipate, Edward's phone buzzed with a message from Casper.

"Just checking in on you, bro. Hope you're not making a mistake with Claire."

Edward frowned at the message, irritation bubbling up again. "It's like he doesn't know when to stop."

Claire rolled her eyes. "Ignore him. He doesn't know what he's talking about. We'll prove him wrong."

"Yeah," Edward replied, determination returning. "I won't let anyone come between us."

In the days that followed, Edward and Claire faced challenges together, confronting misunderstandings and building trust. Casper continued to voice his concerns, but each time, Claire reassured Edward of her commitment.

One afternoon, Casper sat down with Claire to discuss his feelings. "I just want what's best for you," he said, his tone earnest. "Are you sure about Edward?"

Claire sighed, trying to understand. "Casper, I appreciate that you care, but I can take care of myself. Edward makes me happy."

"I know, but it just feels like he might not be the right choice," Casper replied, vulnerability creeping into his voice.

"Why do you think that?" Claire asked, sensing his deeper feelings.

"I just... I don't want to see you get hurt again," he confessed, his frustration evident.

"I understand, but this is different. I feel safe with him, and I trust him," Claire said firmly.

Meanwhile, Ericka watched their conversation unfold, feeling a pang of jealousy. She approached Edward later that day, wanting to get his attention.

"Hey, Edward," she said casually, leaning against the doorframe. "How are things with Claire?"

"It's going well," Edward replied, slightly guarded. "Why do you ask?"

Ericka's tone turned a little too sweet. "Just curious. You know, if things don't work out, I'm always here."

Edward raised an eyebrow. "Thanks, but I'm not looking for anything else right now."

Ericka smiled, masking her disappointment. "Just thought I'd let you know."

As Edward prepared to leave the company, he felt a mix of excitement and apprehension. On his last day, he gathered his colleagues for a small farewell.

"Thank you all for the support over the years," he said, looking around the room. "I'm stepping into a new chapter of my life, and I appreciate everything you've done for me."

Dr. John approached him, clapping a hand on his shoulder. "You're making the right choice, Edward. Enjoy your life."

With Claire by his side, Edward stepped into a future filled with possibilities.

They spent weekends exploring new hobbies, traveling, and deepening their relationship.

Each day felt like a new adventure, one they embraced together.

As the weeks turned into months, Casper began to see the connection between Edward and Claire in a new light.

One evening, he approached them at a gathering.

"Okay, I admit it," he said, holding up his hands. "I was wrong. You two are good together."

Edward smiled, surprised. "Really?"

"Yeah, I see how happy you make her. Just know I'll always be looking out for her," Casper said, a hint of sincerity in his voice.

Claire beamed, relief washing over her. "Thank you, Casper. It means a lot."

Ericka, overhearing the exchange, felt a mix of disappointment and resolve. She decided to confront Edward one last time. "You know, if you ever need someone to talk to, I'm here," she said, trying to sound casual.

"Thanks, Ericka, but I'm really focused on Claire right now," Edward replied, his tone firm.

As the seasons changed, so did their relationships. Edward and Claire continued to grow closer, proving their love to themselves and those around them.

With Casper's reluctant support and Ericka's lingering feelings, they navigated the complexities of friendship and love.

Their love was a testament to resilience, proving that sometimes, the hardest paths lead to the most beautiful destinations.

CHAPTER FIVE

THE SECRET OF TRUTH

In the celestial realms where the ethereal winds whispered secrets of the universe, the Supreme Spirit floated, an embodiment of light and power.

His form shimmered like the dawn, casting a luminescent glow that painted the skies with hope. Yet, within his boundless heart, a yearning had taken root— a love for the Goddess of Peace, Elysia.

Elysia, with her hair like cascading waterfalls and a voice that soothed the stormiest of hearts, represented everything pure and tranquil.

The two had often met in the garden of the cosmos, where flowers bloomed in iridescent hues, and time seemed to hold its breath.

One fateful evening, as the stars twinkled in approval, Elysia looked into the Supreme Spirit's eyes, her own filled with a profound sadness.

"Why do you look at me like that?" she asked, her voice a gentle caress.

"I see a future that can never be ours," he replied, his tone heavy with despair.

"The Book of Fatum has already decreed your fate, binding you to the Vampire Lord."

Elysia sighed, a sound that resonated with the weight of worlds.

"But destiny is cruel. I feel it in my bones, the path laid out for me, yet my heart belongs to you."

The Supreme Spirit reached out, his fingers brushing against hers. "I would challenge the heavens for you. But what is a spirit against fate?"

The Book of Fatum

As whispers of their love reached the ears of the cosmos, the Book of Fatum lay open in its hidden sanctum, inked in the blood of fate. The pages fluttered, revealing the intertwined destinies of Elysia and the Vampire Lord, a bond forged in shadows and light.

In the dim corners of his castle, the Vampire Lord, Valen, stared at his reflection, seeing not a ruler but a broken man.

His past, filled with betrayal and scorn from the ancients, had forged him into a being of darkness, a creature of night who craved vengeance.

"You seek to be free from the pain?" a voice echoed through the shadows— an apparition of his former self.

"Then embrace the darkness."

Valen clenched his jaw.

"The world has wronged me. Elysia deserves better, and I will give her the power she deserves, even if it means tearing down this realm."

As if summoned by his thoughts, a figure cloaked in shadows appeared before him.

It was the Supreme Spirit, his aura radiant despite the gloom surrounding Valen.

"You would doom her to a life of suffering?" the Supreme Spirit challenged, his voice a melodic yet powerful undertone.

Valen smirked, his eyes glinting with malice.

"If I cannot have her, then no one shall.

Not you, not anyone.
I will unleash a darkness upon this world that will make them tremble."

Desperation clawed at the Supreme Spirit's heart as he contemplated his next move.

He sought out the Book of Fatum, standing before its imposing presence, pages swirling like a tempest.

"What must I do to change this fate?" he implored, voice echoing through the void.

A voice, cold and omniscient, replied, "To alter destiny, you must sacrifice what is most precious to you."

The Supreme Spirit felt the weight of his unborn child—a symbol of hope and love.

The thought of giving up his son shattered his soul, yet he could not bear the thought of Elysia suffering at the hands of Valen.

"I accept," he whispered, sealing his fate.

The pages of the Book absorbed his words, the ink swirling like a storm as a pact was formed.

The Supreme Spirit watched in anguish as a piece of his essence was drawn away, a light extinguished forever.

Years passed, and Elysia gave birth to Ada, a child blessed and cursed with powers of both light and dark.

Valen, consumed by his insatiable desire for revenge, abandoned his family, his heart turned to stone.

Elysia, determined to protect Ada from the shadows that loomed over them, often spoke of balance.

"You must understand, my darling," she said, kneeling beside her daughter.

"Your powers are a gift and a burden. Use them wisely."

Ada looked up, confusion knitting her brow.

"But why did Father leave us, Mother? Why does he seek to destroy?"

Elysia sighed, her heart heavy with the truth.

"He is lost in his pain. He believes that by tearing the world apart, he can reclaim his dignity.

But it will only lead to more suffering."

Ada, feeling the weight of her lineage, clenched her fists. "Then I will find him. I will show him that peace is possible."

Meanwhile, in the mortal realm, Dr. Roy paced the dimly lit laboratory, a whirlwind of grief and madness. His vampire wife had perished under tragic circumstances, leaving a void that consumed him.

"I will bring you back, my love," he murmured, pouring over ancient texts and forbidden rituals.

"No matter the cost."

As he experimented, whispers of the Supreme Spirit's son, sealed within a relic, reached his ears.

Legends spoke of its power to alter destinies, and desperation fuelled his resolve.

In the dead of night, he gathered his instruments, preparing to break the relic.

"Forgive me, my love," he whispered, as he plunged into the arcane.

"This world cannot bear your absence any longer."

Ada, following her intuition, ventured into the dark depths of the forest where her father had last been seen. Shadows twisted around her, a testament to the duality within her soul.

"Father!" she called, her voice echoing through the night.

In response, the trees seemed to whisper secrets of his whereabouts, guiding her deeper into the heart of darkness.

Suddenly, a figure emerged— a tall man with eyes as cold as the moonlit sky. It was Valen, his presence heavy with darkness.

"Ada?" he asked, confusion flickering across his face. "What are you doing here?"

"I came to bring you home," she pleaded, her voice trembling.

"Mother misses you. I miss you."

Valen scoffed, his voice laced with bitterness.

"Home? There is no home for me.

The world has made me a monster, and I will make it pay."

"But you can't destroy everything!" Ada cried, her own powers swirling dangerously.

"You don't have to be alone!"

The air crackled with tension as their powers clashed. Ada, embodying both light and dark, stood resolute against her father's darkness.

"You are a part of me, and I will not let you drown in this despair!" she declared, channeling her energy.

Valen hesitated, the weight of her words striking a chord. "You know nothing of pain, child. The world has betrayed me time and time again."

"But I can help you!" she cried, tears shimmering in her eyes.

"Let me show you that there is still beauty in this world."

In that moment, a flicker of the old Valen emerged —a flicker of the man who had once loved Elysia deeply. "You... you could never understand," he said, his voice faltering.

Meanwhile, Dr. Roy's experiments reached a climax as he prepared to break the relic containing the Supreme Spirit's son.

The air thickened with anticipation, energy swirling as he chanted incantations.

As the relic cracked, light poured forth, illuminating the shadows that enveloped his lab.

He gasped as a figure emerged—a being of pure light, radiant and powerful.

"You have released me," the Supreme Spirit's son said, voice echoing like thunder. "But at what cost?"

Dr. Roy, eyes wide with a mix of awe and fear, replied, "I wish to bring back my wife. I am willing to pay any price."

The Supreme Spirit's son studied him, understanding the depths of his despair.

"Love is powerful, but the path you tread is fraught with danger."

"Do you not see the consequences?"

Back in the forest, Ada's plea pierced through Valen's darkness like a beam of light.

"You taught me that love can conquer all, Father. Don't you see? Your rage only leads to more pain."

As their energies clashed, the forest echoed with their struggle. Elysia's spirit hovered nearby, watching, heart aching for her family.

"I will not let my child fall to despair," she whispered, channeling her essence to protect Ada.

The battle raged on, Ada's light pushing against Valen's dark aura.

"I won't give up on you!" she shouted, summoning every ounce of her power.

Valen faltered, memories flooding back— the laughter, the love, the life he had shared with Elysia. The darkness began to wane, a flicker of hope igniting within him.

As the relic shattered, a surge of energy erupted, merging the realms of light and dark. The Supreme Spirit's son stepped forward, sensing the turmoil in the air.

"Enough!" he commanded, and the world seemed to pause.

"Your destinies are intertwined, and only together can you forge a new path."

Valen, torn between his vengeance and the love he felt for his daughter, struggled to find his voice. "Ada... my child, do you truly believe in the possibility of peace?"

Ada nodded fiercely, tears streaming down her cheeks.

"I believe in you, Father. "

"The world may have wronged you, but we can create a future together."

"You don't have to fight alone anymore."

For the first time, Valen felt a crack in the wall of darkness surrounding his heart.

Memories of laughter with Elysia flickered in his mind, intertwining with visions of Ada's bright spirit.

The hatred that had fuelled him began to wane.

"Can I truly escape this cycle?" he murmured, vulnerability seeping into his tone.

"I have brought pain to those I love."

"It's never too late to change," Ada urged, stepping closer, her aura shimmering with light.

"You taught me that true strength lies in the heart. We can heal together."

The Supreme Spirit's son watched, sensing the monumental shift taking place.

"Valen, your choices have led you to this moment. Redemption is possible, but it requires sacrifice—not just of the past, but of the hatred that binds you."

The Vampire Lord's expression twisted in conflict. "And what will become of my revenge? The world will never forgive me."

"Forgiveness begins with you," the Supreme Spirit's son replied, his voice steady.

"You can redefine your legacy. Choose love over hate."

As Valen wrestled with his emotions, the forest around them reacted to his turmoil.

Shadows twisted and curled, reflecting his inner chaos. The once vibrant trees dulled, and the air thickened with uncertainty.

Dr. Roy, deep in his own struggle, felt the shift as the energy from the relic pulsed through his veins.

The realisation of what he had unleashed dawned on him.

"What have I done?" he gasped, his mind racing with horror.

The Supreme Spirit's son turned his attention to the scientist.

"You have disrupted the balance.

You sought to bring back a love lost, but in doing so, you may doom countless others."

Dr. Roy's hands trembled.

"I only wanted to bring her back. I thought... I thought I could fix everything."

"Love cannot be forced back to life through dark means," the Supreme Spirit's son said, the weight of his words settling heavily in the air.

"It requires understanding, acceptance, and sometimes, letting go."

Ada's resolve hardened as she stepped between her father and the encroaching shadows.

"We can face this together, Father. You've faced darkness alone for too long. Let me help you find your way back to the light."

Valen's gaze softened as he looked at Ada, the embodiment of his past and his future.

The darkness around him pulsed with frustration, battling against the burgeoning light within.

"I... I cannot abandon my anger," he whispered, the weight of his past pressing heavily on his shoulders.

"It is all I have left."

"But it isn't all you are," Ada insisted, her voice unwavering.

"You are so much more than your pain. You are a father, a protector. Embrace that."

Valen took a deep breath, feeling the warmth of Ada's light against the coldness of his heart.

"What if I fail again? What if I hurt you?"

"You won't," Ada said, stepping closer. "You have the chance to rewrite your story. Trust in the love that binds us."

In that moment, Valen felt the icy tendrils of vengeance begin to thaw.

The shadows around him flickered, hesitating, sensing their master's changing resolve.

The forest around them began to shift as the relic's energy pulsed through the air.

The Supreme Spirit's son lifted his hand, calling upon the cosmic forces that surrounded them.

"Valen, your sacrifice may be what unites the light and dark," he declared.

"You must be willing to let go of the darkness to forge a new path."

Valen closed his eyes, summoning the strength he had hidden for so long.

"I am tired of being a slave to my anger. If I can protect Ada... if I can protect Elysia's legacy, then I will fight for that."

A surge of energy erupted as Valen extended his hand, and shadows began to dissipate, revealing the vibrant colours of the forest.

The balance of light and dark began to harmonise, creating a new energy.

As the shadows receded, Dr. Roy watched in awe, realising the profound impact of their choices.

"I never wanted to harm anyone. I just wanted to bring back my wife..."

The Supreme Spirit's son turned to him, his gaze piercing.

"You must understand that life and death are part of a cycle. Sometimes, love means allowing those we cherish to rest."

Dr. Roy's heart twisted with regret.

"I am so sorry," he whispered, tears streaming down his face.

"I wish I had realised sooner."

With a sudden clarity, he stepped forward.

"If my actions have harmed anyone, I will make it right.

I will do whatever it takes to restore balance."

The air shimmered with the merging energies of light and dark as Valen and Ada stood united, their bond stronger than ever.

"Let us create a new legacy," Valen declared, his voice resonating with newfound strength. "One of love, not vengeance."

Ada beamed with pride, feeling her father's warmth envelop her.

"Together, we can face whatever comes. The world is ready for change."

In that moment, Dr. Roy felt a powerful surge of energy radiating from the forest. The Supreme Spirit's son nodded, the air around them shimmering.

"Then let it be so."

As Valen and Ada held hands, their powers intertwined, a brilliant light enveloped them.

The darkness that once threatened to consume them transformed into a cascade of vibrant colours, illuminating the forest and beyond.

With the shadows dispelled, the realm breathed a sigh of relief.

Elysia, watching from the ethereal plane, felt a wave of hope wash over her.

"They've done it," she whispered, tears of joy in her eyes.
The forest thrummed with life, and the world began to heal. Valen, Ada, and Dr. Roy stood together, their destinies irrevocably intertwined.

"Together, we will honour the memory of those we've lost," Valen vowed, looking at Ada and Dr. Roy.

"We will build a future where love prevails over hate."

As dawn broke, painting the sky with hues of orange and gold, the Supreme Spirit's son looked on, his heart swelling with pride.

"This is only the beginning. Destiny is malleable, shaped by choices, sacrifices, and love."

Valen turned to his daughter, a smile breaking through the remnants of his past.

"Let's create a world worth fighting for."

Ada nodded, her heart full of determination.

"Together, we'll show the world that peace is possible."

In the days that followed, the bond between Valen and Ada deepened as they worked to mend the rifts in their world.

Guided by Elysia's teachings and the wisdom of the Supreme Spirit's son, they sought to balance light and dark.

Dr. Roy dedicated himself to understanding the true nature of life and death, channeling his grief into knowledge that could help others.

"I will honour my wife by preserving life, not trying to control it," he vowed, finding solace in the love he still held for her.

They ventured through the realms, spreading messages of hope and reconciliation, the shadows of the past faded, replaced by a brighter future.

Valen's reputation transformed from that of a feared vampire lord to a protector, a guardian of peace.

Years passed, and the world flourished under their guidance.

Ada, now a powerful beacon of light, traveled to distant lands, sharing her message of unity.

With each person she inspired, the threads of fate wove a new tapestry, one filled with promise.

Valen, always at her side, found healing in the connections they forged.

He no longer felt the chains of his past; instead, he embraced the possibilities that lay ahead.

In a serene glade, they often reflected on their journey, surrounded by the vibrancy of life.

"Look how far we've come," Ada marvelled, a radiant smile gracing her face.

Valen nodded, pride swelling within him. "It was never just about vengeance. It was about finding the light in the darkness."

One fateful evening, as the stars twinkled above like scattered diamonds, Elysia appeared to them, ethereal and radiant.

"You have done well, my beloved and my daughter," she said, her voice echoing through the glade.

Valen felt tears prick at his eyes as he looked upon Elysia, the love of his life.

"I wished for a chance to make things right. To show you that I could change."

Elysia smiled, her presence enveloping them in warmth. "You have not only changed for yourself but for the world. You have proven that love can conquer even the darkest of paths."

Ada stepped forward, her heart full.

"We carry your legacy with us, Mother. Your teachings guide us every day."

"I see the light you both shine," Elysia said, her voice with a melodic embrace.

CHAPTER SIX

EXECUTION OF THE EVILS

The shadowed corridors of ancient history, a name sends shivers through the marrow of the earth—Morrison. This figure of darkness, a master of sinister formulas, harnessed the very energy of the world, twisting it to seize wealth and dominion. His ambition was a blackened flame, consuming everything in its path, while his cruelty knew no rival. But his rise brought forth a reckoning. Valen recognised the threat Morrison posed.

Their fateful clash was cataclysmic, a battle that tore the fabric of reality. In that moment of reckoning, Valen struck with unparalleled fury, entombing Morrison in stone, forever silencing his malevolent ambitions.

Yet the echoes of Morrison's dark legacy linger, woven into the very fabric of the world. Devoted worshipers continue to venerate him, drawn to the allure of his forbidden power. Deep within the underworld, a cursed sword lies hidden, pulsating with the remnants of his spirit— a weapon that hungers for blood and seeks a new master.

The tale of Morrison endures, a chilling testament to the seductive nature of ambition and the darkness that resides in the hearts of men. As whispers of the sword grow louder, the world braces itself for a *resurgence of chaos, for when the blade is found, it promises to unleash a tempest of darkness unlike any before.*

Amidst the turmoil of a world teetering on the brink of chaos, Wesker stood resolute, his heart a tempest of vengeance.

"I will avenge you, Great-Grandfather," he whispered to the winds, recalling the tales of Morrison's dark legacy that haunted his family. His quest transcended mere retribution; it was a promise.

The stage was set for an epic confrontation, one that intertwined Wesker's fate with the old lady from the Lost and Found.

"You seek to challenge the shadows, young warrior?" she said, her voice a raspy echo of ancient wisdom.

"Only pure souls may enter this realm. Can you bear the weight of your ancestor's sins?"

Wesker's eyes flashed with determination.

"I will not falter. I am his blood."

She studied him, her gaze piercing.

"Then know this: Morrison defied the sanctity of this place, ensnared by dark forces. You tread a dangerous path."

In his hand, Wesker gripped the ancient sword, its hilt cold and heavy with power. As he began the ritual, the air thickened, charged with an energy that crackled around him.

"I call upon the spirits of the past," he intoned, his voice steady. "Unstone the one who was lost!"

Suddenly, the sky split open, and ominous red lightning arced across the heavens. The old lady gasped, her voice trembling with urgency.

"No! What have you done?"

Wesker's resolve hardened. "I have awakened him. Let him return!"

The ground trembled and the darkness swirled, the lady's voice broke through the chaos.

"You do not understand! Morrison comes back not as a man, but as a force of vengeance! The world may not survive his wrath!"

The winds howled in agreement, carrying the weight of her warning.

"It is too late," Wesker replied, his heart pounding. "Let the world face its reckoning."

With those words, the shadows deepened, and the air grew thick with an impending doom. The prophecy of the old lady echoed ominously, and the line between salvation and destruction blurred, as Morrison's laughter rang through the night, heralding his rebirth.

Ada stood beneath the ominous glow of the blood-red moon, a sense of urgency pulsing through her veins. She knew the gravity of their situation; Wesker and Morrison were poised to unleash chaos.

"Father," she called to Valen, "we need to act fast."

Valen's expression was grim.

"I know, Ada. They have the upper hand, but we can't back down. We must prepare for what's coming."

Just then, Edward burst onto the scene, breathless.

"Ada, I heard something crucial. Casper mentioned that Wesker is linked to the old lady from Lost and Found."

"What? You shouldn't be here!" Ada shot back, her concern for Edward clear.

"It's too risky!"

"I don't care! I need to find her," Edward insisted.

"The shop... it's closed."

"Closed? What do you mean? Did anyone see her?" Ada asked, panic rising.

A nearby neighbour interjected, "Yeah, she vanished yesterday. No one knows where she went."

Edward's eyes fell on a letter hanging on the door. "There's a letter here... it's for you, Ada."

Ada carefully unfolded the letter. As she read, her heart sank.

"It's a warning... destruction is coming. We're running out of time."

Valen stepped closer, urgency in his tone.

"We need to figure out Morrison's next move. If we don't, we'll all be caught in the fallout."

"Right. We need to strategize. We can't face this alone," Ada replied, determination flooding her voice.

"*Together*, we stand a chance," Valen added.

"But we must be smart about it."

Edward, resolute, declared, "I'm not backing down. We find that old lady and uncover what Wesker is planning."

Ada nodded, her resolve solidifying.

"Then we work as a team. No more secrets, no more hesitation. We're in this together."said Ada.

The tension in the air was palpable.

Ada's prediction echoed through the quiet room like an omen, heavy and foreboding.

The world was on the brink, and the clock was ticking down to an inevitable confrontation. Morrison's army was growing stronger by the hour, fuelled by the dark powers of the ancient sword, and now the balance of the world rested on a fragile thread.

Ada's voice trembled as she spoke, her eyes distant, "Morrison's attack will come tomorrow. I saw it in my vision. He's bringing everything he has. I don't know if we're ready."

Edward, who had been strategizing with Dr. Roy and Mrs. Smith, now joined her side, his face grim but determined.

"We'll be ready. The people we've gathered... they have the strength. The power to fight."

But Ada's unease didn't waver.

"Even with all of them, it's not enough. We're still dealing with forces that are older than time itself."

Valen, who had been overseeing the preparation of the defences, stepped into the room. His gaze fell upon Ada, his expression soft but heavy with the weight of memories.

"You're worried about Wesker, aren't you?" he asked, his voice quiet, but filled with knowing.

Ada looked up at her father.

"I keep thinking about the past. We were close once. Wesker, Becka, and I. But somewhere along the way, we lost our way."

Valen's eyes clouded with emotion as he looked out into the night.

"You were a child once, Ada. The most powerful of the Upworld, your powers could see into the future, shape destinies. But you were also a child. And that's something Wesker never understood. He was driven by a need to be stronger, to prove something that only led him down a path of destruction."

Ada sighed deeply.

"I never expected him to go this far. We trained together, fought together. And now... now he's an enemy."

Valen patted Ada on the shoulder, his touch firm but reassuring.

"It's a hard truth. But we must face it, and we must fight for what's right. We're the last line of defense."

As the night deepened, Ada stood on the balcony, the cold wind brushing her face.

She couldn't shake the feeling that something far worse was on the horizon. The stars above seemed to flicker and fade as if even the heavens were uncertain of what was to come.

In the underworld, Wesker stood alone in a dark, cavernous hall, the sound of his footsteps echoing in the emptiness. His eyes gleamed with a cold, calculating light, and his mind was consumed with thoughts of Ada. He knew she was coming for him—he could feel her presence in the very air around him, like an electric charge waiting to spark.

"Ada," he whispered to the shadows, his voice a low, sinister murmur.

"You'll miss me, won't you? We'll meet again soon... in a way you never expected."

He stood before a massive altar, his hand resting on the cursed sword that had been the catalyst for this entire chain of events.

It pulsed with dark energy, its blade humming with the remnants of Morrison's power. Wesker had made it his own, binding his will to it, knowing that its return would be the final piece of his ascendancy.

The power it offered was limitless, and he would use it to crush anyone who stood in his way—including Ada and her precious family."Let the world burn," Wesker muttered, his lips curling into a malicious smile.

"Let them come. Let them think they can stop me. Tomorrow... everything changes."

Back in the world above, the gathered forces were making their final preparations.

The 78 people with unique abilities, each empowered by their own stone, stood ready.

The red stones— Ada, the blue stone—Edward, and the black stone —Valen held —had long been the symbols of their power, but now they would be tested as never before.

Their abilities were vast and varied, but none of them had ever faced an army as powerful as Morrison's or an enemy as dangerous as Wesker.

Mrs. Smith and Dr. Roy were organising the defence points, working tirelessly to ensure the vampires in their network were in position, while also strengthening the protective shields around key locations. They had gathered forces from across the globe —warriors from every corner of the earth, gifted with the power to manipulate the elements: earth, wind, water, fire.

Yet even they were unsure if they had the strength to survive what was coming.

Valen had traveled far to rally those with similar abilities, especially those gifted with foresight and elemental power.

He'd even managed to find people who could manipulate time, bending it in subtle ways to create advantages in battle.

Edward, meanwhile, had reached out to his network, gathering warriors with the ability to control objects, bend air, and teleport from one place to another.

There were also those who could inflict pain with a mere glance, others who could shape-shift or manipulate shadows.

It was a vast and varied army, but their powers were untested against the forces Morrison commanded.

As the night wore on, Ada gathered the group of warriors at her house, preparing them for the final stand. Her heart was heavy, her mind clouded with visions of what was to come. In one such vision, she saw Edward standing still in the middle of a battlefield, the red stone in his hand glowing with a strange light. In that vision, an antidote sat by his side, and it was clear to Ada that if the stone left its possession —if she let it fall —it would be her death.

The vision lingered in her mind, haunting her.

"This isn't just about saving the world," she muttered to herself.

"It's about saving us all... even if it costs everything."

Valen approached her once more, noticing the concern etched in her expression. He knew his daughter well. "Ada... you look like you're carrying the weight of the world on your shoulders."

She looked up at him, eyes filled with a mixture of determination and sorrow.

"I am. But I'll carry it. For all of us."

Valen nodded, his face hardening with resolve.

"Then we fight together.

We've always fought together."

The battle was **imminent**.

Tomorrow would bring chaos, and the world would never be the same. Ada, Valen, and Edward knew that they had only one chance to stop Morrison, to stop Wesker—and to prevent the apocalypse that loomed just on the horizon.

As the night deepened, the world held its breath.

Morrison's voice thundered across the battlefield, cutting through the chaos like a blade. His words were both a challenge and a declaration, and they ignited a fiery tremor in the hearts of his followers.

"Tonight, we are gathered here, for tomorrow— for revenge, and for ruling the world. I am Morrison, the foremost God you shall pray to."

The ground trembled beneath him, and the very air seemed to crackle with a palpable darkness. Morrison stood tall, his form a terrifying mix of mortal cunning and vampire strength— an indestructible force, a hybrid god that would not be denied.

His eyes, glowing with ancient malice, swept over the battlefield, and every man, woman, and beast before him bowed in reverence, compelled by his overwhelming presence.

He was the apex of destruction, and he knew it.

"Let them come," he sneered, his voice carrying the weight of centuries of hatred and ambition.

"They will fall before me. The world will kneel, and it will belong to me. Forever."

Ada's heart pounded in her chest as she watched from a distance, her eyes locked on the twisted vision of power that Morrison had become.

Ada's mind raced as she caught sight of Wesker standing in the distance, his expression cold and unreadable.

Stop it, Wesker, she thought desperately.

This can't get any worse.

But Wesker's voice, like a knife cutting through her thoughts, echoed back.

"Surrender, Ada. I don't want you to get involved in this. You could get hurt."

"What about the world, Wesker?!"

Ada shot back, her voice rising with urgency.

"We can't just let them die. Have faith in God —not in the army made by this Lord!"

"It's too late to stop it now," Wesker muttered.

The relic before them pulsed with dark energy, showing the first vision to Morrison:

If you don't stop now, you'll lose everything.

But Morrison ignored it.

The battlefield stretched before her like a scene from a nightmare.

On one side stood Morrison's dark legion —an army of monsters, demons, and corrupted souls, each one fuelled by his curse. On the other, Valen's army of 78 warriors gathered, standing tall against the tide of darkness. The stakes couldn't be higher.

This was the day the world would be decided.

Ada's thoughts raced as Dr. Roy's voice echoed in her mind, the memory of their conversation still fresh.

"This is how we lost your grandfather," he had said softly, his face grim.

"Morrison is invincible unless you have the Vampire Stone. Only that can defeat him.

But it has to be perfect. The stone must be perfectly aligned, and the shot must be direct. If it's not…"

Ada's throat tightened at the thought.

"If it's not, Morrison will absorb its power," she had murmured, the weight of the situation sinking in.

"He'll become unstoppable."

Dr. Roy's voice had been heavy with sorrow.

"Exactly. And the stone…" "It's a legend now. A myth. Impossible to find. You might have a better chance of reaching the heavens than finding that stone."

But now, standing on the precipice of war, Ada knew there was no turning back.

There was only one option, and she had to take it. She had to stop Morrison.

"Then I'll find it,"she muttered to herself, clenching her fists.

"I'll find it, and I'll end this."

The sky overhead began to churn with dark clouds, and the first clash of the armies erupted like a thunderstorm. The earth shook as Zaf, a warrior of the earthen stone, slammed his hands into the ground, causing the very ground to split beneath Morrison's army.

Rocks, boulders, and jagged earth flew into the air as the ground itself rebelled.

"You'll never have this world!"

Zaf shouted, his voice filled with raw power as the ground swallowed hundreds of Morrison's forces.

Yura, a sorceress of water stone, was quick to follow.

She raised her hands, and with a single motion, a massive wave surged from the river, crashing into Morrison's army.

The wave tore through the ranks, drowning demons and creatures alike in its violent embrace.

"This is the power of the oceans!"

Yura cried out, her voice a fierce declaration as she watched the tide of destruction roll over her enemies.

But Morrison, undeterred, raised his hands, and the very air seemed to darken around him.

The ground trembled as a pulse of dark energy erupted from him, nullifying Zaf's efforts and pushing back the waves of water. The battlefield seemed to quiver under the weight of his power.

"Your efforts are futile," Morrison snarled, his eyes burning with an ancient fury. "Nothing will stand against me. The world is mine!"

The storm above them raged with chaos as "Luke", the wind stone master, took to the skies.

His body swirled with the wind, and with a mighty roar, he unleashed a tempest so fierce that it ripped through Morrison's forces like a blade.

Demons and soldiers alike were sent flying, crashing into one another with bone-crushing force.

"The storm is here, Morrison!"

Luke yelled, his voice a primal howl.

Yet, no matter how much chaos they unleashed, Morrison stood firm, his power an impenetrable wall. "This world is mine to take, and nothing will stop me," he declared, his voice growing in intensity as he waved his hand, dispelling the storm with a single motion.

In the thick of the battle, Edward found himself facing Wesker— a fight that had been inevitable.

The two of them had once fought side by side, but now, they were enemies.

Their swords clashed with a resounding crack, each strike sending shockwaves through the air.

Edward's strength was great, but Wesker's was overwhelming, and with each passing moment, he felt himself being pushed back.

"You're too weak, Edward," Wesker taunted, his voice cold as ice.

"You never understood the true power of the dark forces we're dealing with."

Edward gritted his teeth, parrying Wesker's blows. "You've lost your way, Wesker. You're no better than Morrison."

His sword swung in a flash of steel, but Wesker effortlessly blocked it, his smirk never faltering.

"You still don't get it, do you?

This is about survival. The world doesn't care about heroes, Edward. Only power matters now."

Edward's eyes flashed with anger.

"I care about the world! And I'll fight to save it, no matter the cost!"

But before he could react, *Ada* stepped forward, her eyes glowing with radiant light.

She raised a hand, and a shimmering barrier surrounded Edward, blocking Wesker's next attack.

"That's enough, Wesker!"

Ada's voice rang out with authority.

"This madness ends now."

Wesker's gaze shifted toward her, and for the briefest of moments, there was something like hesitation in his eyes.

But it was gone in an instant, replaced with cold indifference.

"You think you can stop me, Ada?,"he scoffed.

"You're just as naïve as Edward."

"I've had enough of your lies, Wesker!" Ada shouted, her voice rising with fury.

With a powerful wave of her hand, she sent a shockwave rippling through the air, knocking Wesker off his feet.

"I'm not the one who's lost their way. You are."

The battle raged on around them, but it was clear that they couldn't defeat Morrison without the Vampire Stone.

Ada's mind was already racing, her thoughts consumed with the ancient artefact.

"I have to find it. I have to end this," she thought, her eyes darting to the horizon where the stone was said to be hidden —her only hope.

But then, in the midst of it all, a vision struck her like a lightning bolt. It wasn't just a vision of victory—it was a vision of herself, standing before Morrison with the stone in her hand, knowing that the cost would her life.

"Your soul will be the price," a voice whispered in her mind, and her heart clenched with fear.

"No," she whispered, the weight of the decision sinking in.

"I can't do it. I can't..."

But Dr. Roy's voice echoed in her mind.

"You must, Ada. If you are to save the world, you must act. You are the key."

Edward, sensing her hesitation, rushed to her side.

"Ada, no! You don't have to do this! There has to be another way!"

But Wesker, ever the manipulator, whispered, his voice cold and sinister.

"I can't let you do this, Ada. You're too young to die."

Ada turned toward him, her expression unwavering.

"It's the only way, Wesker.

The world needs to be saved.

And if it costs me everything... then that's the price I'll pay."

Edward's heart broke as he watched her reach for the stone around her neck.

"No, Ada!" he cried, but she had already made up her mind.

With a trembling hand, Ada crushed the stone in her palm.

The world seemed to hold its breath as an explosion of pure light erupted from her body, sending shockwaves through the battlefield. Everything around them seemed to freeze.

I am the sacrifice," she whispered, knowing that she had become the key to their salvation.

Morrison, sensing the power, turned toward her.

"No! You will not stop me!" he roared, but the pieces of Ada's shattered stone, along with the Vampire Stone, collided in midair, sending a massive shockwave that ripped through the fabric of reality itself.

The energy was overwhelming, tearing through Morrison's army and pulling the forces of the vampire realm back into their respective stones.

In the chaos, Morrison let out a scream of fury, but it was too late. With a final, earth-shattering explosion of energy, he fell to the ground, his body crumbling to dust as his army disintegrated around him.

As the smoke cleared, Wesker and Edward rushed to Ada's side, their hearts heavy with fear and hope.

"Ada!" Edward cried, his voice trembling.

"Ada, please..."

The moment Ada crushed the stone, a blinding light engulfed her, so brilliant that it seemed to erase the very darkness around them.

For a fraction of a second, everything went silent —the world itself holding its breath.

Even Morrison, whose power had been unparalleled, faltered, his eyes wide in disbelief as the energy swirled around Ada, lifting her off the ground.

The very air crackled with an ancient, raw power, and as the light began to recede, Ada stood there, transformed. Her body shimmered with an ethereal glow, her eyes now glowing with the intensity of a thousand stars. The stone, now nothing more than dust in her hand, had merged with her soul.

Ada... no...”

Edward whispered, his voice filled with both awe and fear. He reached out, as if to stop her, but he could feel the overwhelming energy emanating from her. There was no turning back now.

Morrison, now seeing the full extent of what Ada had done, sneered, his lips curling into a wicked smile.

“So, you think this is your salvation?

You are nothing more than a sacrifice, Ada.

You have sealed your own fate, and the world with it.”

But Ada's voice was calm, even as the immense power surged through her veins.

“You're wrong, Morrison. This is the end for you.”

The energy around her twisted, crackling like a storm, and she lifted her hand toward him.

The battlefield around them seemed to bend and warp as the stone's power surged through her, pulling on the very fabric of reality.
The ground beneath them shook again, but this time it was not Morrison's dark energy —it was Ada's.

"You've made one fatal mistake," Ada continued, her voice now resonating with the power of the Vampire Stone.

"You underestimated the sacrifice.

The cost was not just mine to bear —it is the world's, and I am its guardian now."

Her hand stretched out, and the ground beneath Morrison cracked wide open, pulling him down into a vortex of light and shadow.

He fought against it, summoning all his strength, but Ada's newfound power was too great. The very air around them began to hum with the pulse of life and death, an unstoppable force.

"I am the price," she whispered, and in a final act of will, she cast a beam of pure, radiant energy from her outstretched hand.

The light pierced through Morrison's defences, his body disintegrating as the stone's energy consumed him.

Morrison screamed, a howl of rage and despair, as he was torn apart, the darkness that had surrounded him now turning to dust.

The last remnants of his power dissipated, leaving behind nothing but an empty void.

For a moment, everything was still.

The battlefield, once filled with chaos and bloodshed, was silent. The armies of both sides had stopped, watching in awe as Ada hovered above the earth, her glow fading slowly as the power of the Vampire Stone began to stabilize.

Edward, unable to speak for a moment, finally found his voice.

"Ada…" he whispered, taking a step forward, his heart aching as he saw the toll the power had taken on her.

Ada's eyes, now flickering with exhaustion, met his.

"It's done," she said softly, her voice heavy with the weight of what had transpired. "It's over… but at a cost."

The ground beneath her began to tremble, the power she had unleashed now draining away, and with it, her strength.

Slowly, she began to fall, her body no longer able to support the overwhelming energy coursing through her. Edward rushed to catch her, holding her close as she collapsed into his arms.

"Ada… no…" Edward whispered, his voice breaking.

But Ada smiled weakly, her gaze peaceful.

"It was the only way, Edward," she murmured, her breathing shallow.

"The world is saved… but I won't be here to see it."

A tear slipped down Edward's cheek as he held her tighter.

"I'm so sorry… I never wanted this for you."

Ada shook her head slightly, her smile still soft.

"You didn't do this. This was my choice. My *sacrifice*."

Her eyes began to fade, her body growing colder in his arms, but there was a sense of peace within her.

She had given everything for the world, and she was content with that.

"Tell them... tell them I did this for them."

Edward nodded, choking back his tears.

"I will. I swear it."

Ada's body grew still, her heart stilled in his hands.

The battlefield was silent, save for the winds that whispered across the land, the calm after the storm.

The war was over. Morrison was gone.

The world had been saved

—but at the greatest cost.

And in the silence, Edward vowed that he would honour her sacrifice. The world would remember Ada's name, not as a mere legend, but as the one who had given everything to save it. The world was free, but Ada's soul would remain entwined with it forever, her light forever etched in the hearts of those who would carry on her legacy.

As the first rays of dawn broke across the horizon, the battle-weary warriors stood in silence, watching the final act of a hero —one who had given everything, and who would never be forgotten.

Morrison, sensing the raw surge of power, turned toward Ada with eyes wide in disbelief. The very ground seemed to tremble beneath his feet as the energy around her reached a boiling point.

"No! You will not stop me!" he roared, his voice cracking with desperation.

His fingers curled around the hilt of his blade, his dark aura flaring as he prepared to unleash the full force of his power.

But it was too late.

The shattered pieces of Ada's stone, now fused with the Vampire Stone, collided midair in a blinding flash. The resulting shockwave tore through the fabric of reality itself—time and space seemed to twist and ripple as if the universe itself was recoiling. The explosion of energy was deafening, sending a gust of wind so powerful it knocked Morrison off his feet, ripping through his ranks and scattering his forces like paper in a storm. His vampire soldiers cried out in agony as they were sucked into the air, their forms pulled back toward the stones they had once emerged from. The very laws of nature seemed to fracture.

In the chaos, Morrison's fury rose to a scream, but his words were drowned out by the sound of destruction. "No! NO!" He raised his hands toward the sky, summoning all his strength to fight back. But it was too late.

With a final, earth-shattering explosion of pure energy, the destructive force crushed Morrison's dark aura, and he staggered, unable to maintain his form. His body began to disintegrate as if the light itself was burning him from the inside out. The ground cracked open beneath him, and with a cry of pure rage, he crumbled to dust, his final scream fading into nothingness. His army, once a formidable force, followed suit, vanishing into nothingness as the energies pulled them back into the abyss they had been summoned from.

The battlefield was silent for a brief moment, the air thick with the aftermath of a cataclysmic event. Then, the wind began to calm, leaving only the soft hum of the world adjusting to its new reality.

Edward, heart pounding, rushed to Ada's side, his fear and hope warring inside him. He dropped to his knees beside her, trembling hands hovering over her body, feeling the coldness of death that clung to her.

"Ada!" he cried, his voice cracking.

"Ada, please..."

He reached out, trying to touch her, but Valen, his face ashen and grim, stepped forward, his eyes heavy with sorrow.

"She's gone," Valen said quietly, his voice breaking as he looked at Ada's lifeless form.

"Her stone is shattered... and with it, her soul."

Edward shook his head in denial, his breath coming in ragged gasps.

"No! She can't be gone!" he protested, his hands clutching Ada's limp body in desperation.

"There has to be a way... Please, we can't lose her!"

Valen's gaze hardened, his features tight with the weight of truth.

"There is no way. She made her choice."

His voice was low, filled with finality.

"The cost was too great. The stone, the power—it was always meant to take everything."

Wesker, who had been standing at a distance, eyes narrowed in thought, finally spoke, his voice heavy with grief yet tinged with urgency.

"We need to take her to the old mansion.

Tonight... the lunar eclipse is our last chance."

The mansion was a relic, white as bone and eerily silent. It stood waiting, as though prepared for this moment. The eclipse, a rare celestial event that occurred once every 3,000 years, had begun. The wind howled around them, carrying dust and shadows, as the red moon bathed the world in an unnatural glow.

The journey to the mansion was long, and the atmosphere was thick with tension. As they reached the mansion's threshold, the red moon hung ominously in the sky, its glow casting an eerie light across the desolate landscape. The wind howled around them, carrying dust and shadows, and the air was thick with an unnatural chill. They moved quickly, carrying Ada's lifeless form inside the mansion, its white bones-like walls seeming to absorb the very essence of life itself.

The moment they crossed the threshold, the eclipse began. The sky darkened as the shadow of the earth overtook the sun, and a deep, unsettling energy filled the air. The red moon bathed the world in an ominous glow, its rays cutting through the darkness like bloodstained fingers. Time itself seemed to stretch as they set Ada's body on the cold, stone altar at the heart of the mansion.

Wesker turned to Edward, his face hard with determination but tinged with sorrow.

"Give me her necklace," he commanded.

"We need the pieces. We must complete the ritual before the eclipse ends."

Edward, his hands shaking, unclasped the broken necklace, its once-perfect chain now shattered, the red stone fractured and dull.

It had been an ancient relic, once thought lost to time, only rediscovered at the precise moment when the world was on the brink of collapse.

This was the final key.

With trembling hands, Edward placed the shattered necklace into Ada's still hand, the weight of the moment pressing down on him.

Her body lay cold and pale before him, her features tranquil yet lifeless. The eerie wind howled through the broken windows of the mansion, carrying with it the distant sound of wolves' howls —an echo from another time, another realm.

Wesker's voice cut through the silence.

"Do it, Edward. The ritual must proceed. The eclipse is at its peak."

Edward, his heart heavy, nodded, though his body felt as though it were made of stone. With a final, decisive motion, he extended his hand toward Ada's body. As his palm hovered above her, the broken pieces of the necklace began to stir, drawn toward the invisible force that pulsed in the air.

They rose, hovering above his hand, spinning in a chaotic whirl before shooting toward Ada, the shards fusing together in a burst of blinding light.

The pieces of the necklace reformed, the red stone now glowing with an eerie, supernatural radiance. The air itself seemed to vibrate with energy as Ada's body, tethered to the forces of the cosmos, began to rise slowly from the stone altar. It was as if she were suspended between two worlds, her body floating above the ground, her white dress billowing like a spectre. The very air shimmered, bending around her as rings of swirling red energy formed in a circle, surrounding her like a protective, yet destructive force.

The mansion trembled with the force of the ritual.

The walls groaned and creaked, the windows rattling violently. It felt as if the very bones of the earth were being shaken by an unstoppable force.

Outside, the winds howled louder, resonating with a deep, primal sound that seemed to come from the bowels of the earth itself.

Wesker, eyes alight with dark satisfaction, watched as the ritual unfolded, knowing this was the culmination of everything he had worked for.

But as the eclipse reached its peak, something shifted in the air. The wind intensified, the wolves' howls outside growing more frenzied. The air was charged with something beyond their understanding, and Wesker's sense of urgency grew.

"Edward," he said, voice tight with urgency, "open your hand."

Edward complied, his palm outstretched toward Ada. The broken pieces of the necklace that had just fused began to stir again, rising as though pulled by an invisible force.

They hovered above his hand, spinning wildly before they shot back toward Ada. In a flash of light, the necklace became whole, its red stone now pulsing with an otherworldly energy.

Ada's body, suspended in mid-air, began to flicker, as though she were caught between two realms.

Her form seemed to swell with the energy of the cosmos, her very being vibrating with a power far beyond what she had ever known. But as the eclipse reached its final moment, something went wrong. Ada's descent back to the ground was slow, graceful, but unnatural. Her body drifted like a fallen angel, her once-vibrant form now cold and lifeless, though the necklace
—whole once more

—clung to her neck, glowing brightly.

Wesker's gaze narrowed, a frown creasing his face as he watched her form.

"She is not waking," he muttered under his breath.

"Why is she not waking?"

Valen, stepping forward, his voice filled with gravity, spoke softly but resolutely.

"We have to leave her. She is not yet whole. Her soul must be united with her body, and that will take time."

Wesker's lips curled into a sneer, his impatience rising. "Time is a luxury we do not have, Valen. She must awaken now!"

But Valen stood firm, his gaze unyielding.

"No. You do not understand. She is not just Ada anymore. She is something more now. Her soul is fractured. It will take time to heal... to reconnect."

Wesker looked at Ada one last time, his eyes flickering with a mix of satisfaction and frustration.

His plan had worked, but not in the way he had hoped. Ada, now more than vampire, was no longer simply a vampire.

She was something new. The world, it seemed, was shifting around her.

With a final glance, Wesker turned and walked toward the door.

"We leave now," he said coldly, the weight of his words heavy in the air. The door slammed shut behind them, leaving Ada's still form alone in the dark, her body lying in silence.

But in the shadows, something stirred.

A figure stepped forward

—*Becka*, the mysterious force who had watched over Ada's fate from the beginning. Her presence filled the room with an undeniable power, as though she were the embodiment of something ancient and far more vast than they could comprehend.

She approached Ada, her eyes filled with a quiet, unsettling knowing.

Kneeling beside her, she whispered something into the stillness—words meant only for Ada, spoken in a language that no one could hear.

Becka's lips brushed Ada's ear as she spoke softly, almost tenderly.

"We will have a long talk after your end," she murmured. "When you awaken, Ada, you will understand what I have done. But until then, rest. For what comes next will be beyond your comprehension."

With that, Becka rose, vanishing into the shadows like a spectre, leaving the room as silent as death itself.

The mansion, once a place of faded grandeur, now stood as the cradle for something new

—something unknown.

The first rays of the rising sun filtered through the shattered windows, but it did little to illuminate the darkness that clung to the air.

Time passed, and then

—like a whisper from the depths of the ocean

—a shift occurred.

Ada's body began to stir.

Her fingers twitched. Her chest rose and fell with a tentative breath. And then, her eyes fluttered open.

At first, there was nothing but darkness.

But then—her eyes snapped open, and they glowed with the eerie, unnatural red of the blood moon.

For a moment, it felt as though the very world had stopped, as if it were waiting for something far greater.

But that red light faded as quickly as it had appeared. It was replaced by something more unsettling

—something more vast. Her eyes, once red and warm, were now a deep oceanic blue, cold and unfeeling. They seemed to hold the entire world within them, a vastness that sent a chill through the bones of anyone who might have witnessed it.

A mischievous smile tugged at her lips

—a smile that was not Ada's.

This was no longer the woman they had known.

Ada stood slowly, the air around her seeming to recoil from her presence.

The world itself felt heavy, as though something far older than time had stirred within her.

And as she lifted her head, the ocean's call echoed through her, pulling her toward the unknown.

"Had the world changed.... or had she?"

Fall Of Ocean

About The Author

Fatema Mufaddal Saify, born on 13th of October 2007, in Bhopal, India, is an emerging science fiction author with a keen interest in exploring speculative worlds and futuristic concepts. Her passion for the genre stems from its ability to challenge traditional ideas and spark imagination, which deeply influences her own writing.

Alongside her literary pursuits, Fatema is an accomplished visual artist, specialising in nature and abstract art. At the age of 14, she held her first successful exhibition titled "My City", which explored the intricate relationship between urban landscapes and natural elements. Her work has since continued to evolve, reflecting her profound appreciation for both the environment and artistic expression.

Additionally, Fatema is an adept elocutionist, honing her public speaking skills and embracing opportunities for personal expression through speech. With her diverse talents in writing, art, and communication, Fatema Saify exemplifies a dynamic and creative spirit, inspiring others through her innovative approach to art and storytelling.

Masters And Their Stone Of Power

Ada- Red stone
Edward- NavyBlue stone
Velan- Black stone
Zaf- Green stone
Yura- Off white stone
Luke- Teal blue stone

Thank You,

Thank you for joining Ada on her extraordinary journey into the unknown. Writing her story has been a fascinating exploration of what it means to be human, to transcend boundaries, and to face the darkness both within and beyond us.

To my family, friends, and all who have supported me—your unwavering belief in me, even during the most fantastical twists of this tale, has been my anchor. Your encouragement has been my guiding light through every chapter. To my readers, your curiosity and willingness to dive into the shadows with Ada is what truly brings this world to life. I hope her story has challenged your perceptions, sparked your imagination, and perhaps even made you question what lies beneath the surface of our own reality. This journey with Ada may be over for now, but the adventure is far from finished. I look forward to sharing more tales from this world, and exploring even magical corners of the unknown together.

Until we meet again in the next part,

Fatema M Saify